PUFFIN CANADA

ROYAL RANSOM

Eric Walters is the author of twenty-six acclaimed and bestselling novels for children and young adults. His novels have won numerous awards, including the Silver Birch, Blue Heron, Red Maple, Snow Willow and Ruth Schwartz awards, and have received honours from the Canadian Library Association Book Awards and UNESCO's international award for Literature in Service of Tolerance.

Eric resides in Mississauga with his wife, Anita, and children, Christina, Nicholas and Julia. When not writing or touring across the country speaking to school groups, Eric spends time playing or watching soccer and basketball, or playing the saxophone.

To find out more about Eric and his novels, or to arrange for him to speak at your school, visit his website at **www.interlog.com/~ewalters**.

Also by Eric Walters from Penguin Canada

Other books by Eric Walters

ROYAL RANSOM

ERIC WALTERS

PUFFIN
CANADA

PUFFIN CANADA

Penguin Group (Canada), a division of Pearson Penguin Canada Inc.,
10 Alcorn Avenue, Toronto, Ontario M4V 3B2

Penguin Group (U.K.), 80 Strand, London WC2R 0RL, England
Penguin Group (U.S.), 375 Hudson Street, New York, New York 10014, U.S.A.
Penguin Group (Australia) Inc., 250 Camberwell Road, Camberwell, Victoria 3124, Australia
Penguin Group (Ireland), 25 St. Stephen's Green, Dublin 2, Ireland
Penguin Books India (P) Ltd, 11, Community Centre, Panchsheel Park,
New Delhi – 110 017, India
Penguin Group (New Zealand), cnr Rosedale and Airborne Roads, Albany, Auckland 1310,
New Zealand
Penguin Books (South Africa) (Pty) Ltd, 24 Sturdee Avenue, Rosebank 2196, South Africa

Penguin Group, Registered Offices: 80 Strand, London WC2R 0RL, England

First published in Puffin Canada hardcover by Penguin Group (Canada),
a division of Pearson Penguin Canada Inc., 2003
Published in this edition, 2004

1 2 3 4 5 6 7 8 9 10 (OPM)

NATIONAL LIBRARY OF CANADA CATALOGUING IN PUBLICATION

Walters, Eric, 1957–
Royal Ransom / Eric Walters.

ISBN 0-14-331214-6 (bound).—ISBN 0-14-331205-7 (pbk.)

I. Title.

PS8595.A598R69 2003   jC813'.54   C2002-904373-5
                         PZ7

Visit the Penguin Group (Canada) website at **www.penguin.ca**

*For the teachers, librarians and
teacher/librarians who foster the love of reading*

CHAPTER ONE

"JAMIE, WAKE UP!" my grandmother said as she shook me out of a solid sleep.

Before I could even think to say anything my still-shut eyes were hit by piercing light as I heard the *whiz* of my blind shooting up. I pulled the covers over my head.

"Hurry up, Jamie."

"What time is it?" I asked sleepily.

"Time to get up."

"I figured that's what you *think,* but what time *is* it?" I asked as I peeked out.

"How should I know?" She shrugged her shoulders. "It's not like I ever owned a watch."

"But we do have a clock," I pointed out.

"And you have one of those fancy computer things, and that satellite TV thing, and that microphone oven—"

"Micro*wave* oven," I said.

"Whatever it's called. I'm not going to be using any of them anytime soon either," she argued. "I'm not sure if there's room in this house for all those newfangled things and this old woman."

"There's plenty of space for all of you," I said.

It had been almost two months since my grandmother—my mother's mother—moved in with us.

And two months before that my grandfather had died. My grandparents had lived just three doors down, so it wasn't like I hadn't seen them every single day of my life. Still, it had taken a lot of convincing to get my grandmother to move in. She said she didn't want "to get underfoot." She finally agreed only because my mother said she'd be doing *us* a favour. Between my father being away flying charter groups in and out and my mother working on her art, she said it would be helpful to have her around to take care of the house, and me. So she and her things moved into our place.

"Maybe I could just go back to sleep for a *little* while," I suggested.

"Back to sleep!" she snorted. "You've already wasted the best part of the day. The sun has been up in the sky for hours already."

"That doesn't mean much. This time of year the sun is almost always up."

"Either way, you're awake, so you might as well get up!"

My grandmother reached down, grabbed the covers and pulled them off. I was still tired and really wanted to sleep, but I knew that wasn't going to happen. Reluctantly I climbed out of bed.

"Besides, you have work to do," she told me.

"Work?" I asked hesitantly.

She nodded. "I thought you might want to help do some work with your cousin Kenny."

"I might *want* to do lots of things, but working with Kenny isn't one of them," I said.

"Kenny needs your help."

"All I know is that helping Kenny usually means me *working* and him *watching* me work."

My grandmother gave me a small smile. She knew that what I had said was true, but she would never say a bad word about a relative. And when almost everybody in the whole village is related to you in one way or another, that meant that I'd never heard her say a bad word about anybody.

"So just what are Kenny and me doing together?" I asked.

"Cutting some wood."

"We already have all the wood we'll need for next winter!" Most of it I'd cut and stacked myself, so I knew exactly how much we had.

"Didn't say it was for us," my grandmother said.

"So Kenny's going to watch me cut *his* wood?" I protested.

"Didn't say it was for him either."

"Then who?"

"Auntie Francie."

"Auntie Francie! Kenny and me . . . mostly me . . . we already put in all the wood she'll need for next winter."

"She said she needs more wood. She likes to keep the place real warm."

"Couldn't she just put on another sweater?"

"You feel the cold more when you get older because your blood isn't as thick," my grandmother said. "Do you want the poor old woman to feel cold?"

What was I supposed to say to that?

My Auntie Francie, who was my grandmother's oldest sister, lived in a little house at the edge of town. She had no electricity, and her place was heated by wood and lit by oil lamps. Kenny and I had already worked for two whole days to put wood up for her. We'd done maybe ten face cords. That should have been more than enough to heat a place twice as big as her house for the whole winter.

"I heard from Kenny's mother that *he* didn't complain about helping out again," my grandmother said.

"That's because he hasn't actually done anything yet," I argued. Kenny had spent most of the time driving his four-wheeler, bringing back the wood I'd split or "scouting" new stands to be cut. It was amazing how he could keep out of sight until the work was finished.

"The more you argue about work, the less time you have to eat before you go."

"I'm not arguing," I argued.

"Oh, so you're looking for a fight. Now just go and eat your breakfast before Kenny arrives. I'll fix you something."

"Where's Mom?" I asked.

"Took her sketchbook and went out hours ago."

"Sounds like everybody's up except me," I said. "What have you been up to?"

"Dusting. Arranging. Sorting."

"Again?"

"Got lots of things to take care of," she said.

Of course when my grandmother moved in she brought with her a lot of her things. And of all her things, her most prized possession was her "collection." My grandmother collected memorabilia of the Royal Family. She had books and spoons and posters and plates and little statues and magazines and videos. Everywhere you looked, there was an image of somebody in an evening gown and crown or tiara staring back at you.

Even though it didn't do anything for me, I had to admit that it was a pretty amazing assortment of stuff. Of course it would have been even more amazing if it had been something that was the least bit interesting. My grandmother had to be the only Native Canadian in the whole country who was so fascinated by the Royal Family. It all began more than thirty years ago, when her husband—my grandfather—was hired as a guide for a couple of "Royals" for a canoe trip. They gave my grandmother the first piece in her collection: a signed picture of the King of England and his son. It was framed and hung over her bed. She always used to say that if her house ever caught fire she'd grab that picture first, her family photo albums next and my grandfather third.

There was a knock at the door.

"You get that and I'll grab you something quick to eat," my grandmother said.

There was more knocking. Kenny wasn't usually that anxious to start working.

"Hold on, Kenny, I'm coming!" I yelled out. "What's the big . . ?" I stopped mid-sentence as I opened the door. It wasn't Kenny, it was Ray, one of my other cousins.

"You really thinking you might see Kenny up this early?" Ray asked.

"I don't even know what time it is," I answered.

"Around six-thirty."

"I thought it was later," I said. "He's coming here and we're going to go cut some wood for Auntie Francie."

"That should be fun," Ray said. "I've been out cutting wood with that guy half a dozen times and I don't think I've ever seen him lift an axe. I'm not even sure he knows which side of it to sink into the wood."

"I just thought that was how he was with me."

"That's how he is with everybody. If he put half as much effort into working as he does avoiding work he'd be something to watch," Ray said. "You really want to go out with him?"

"I don't want to, but I don't think I have much choice."

"Ah . . . now that's where you're wrong," Ray said with a smile.

"Go on."

"I'm bringing some people out on a canoe trip and I need an extra guide."

"What about Aylmer?" I asked. Aylmer was, of course, another one of our cousins and the person who usually accompanied Ray on these trips.

"He's not feeling so good this morning."

"Does he have that bug that's been going around?" I asked.

Ray laughed. "Only bug that's bothering him is the one that was in the bottle of tequila that he drank last night. So can you come with me?"

"I don't know," I answered.

"What's wrong with going on a little canoe trip?"

"You don't go on little canoe trips. How many days are you going for?" I asked.

"It's short," he said.

"Short like two weeks?"

"No, no, it's only a five-day trip. We're not going too far, either. There's a couple of kids coming along."

"Kids?"

"One about your age and the other a couple years younger."

"And is that supposed to make it better for me?" I asked.

"Sure, why not?"

"It's just that there's not much that's more annoying than rich people's kids. They all seem to act like they're little princes and princesses."

"These kids might be different. So, you in?"

"Five days isn't so bad, although that's still four more days than it's going to take me to cut wood with Kenny."

"You mean for *you* to have Kenny watch you cut wood."

"Either way, if I stay, then tomorrow I'm all through."

"Come on, Jamie, I'm talking about paddling a canoe, not cutting wood."

"Breaking your back chopping wood isn't that much different from breaking your back paddling."

"There is one big difference."

"And what's that?" I asked.

"Nobody's going to pay you for doing the wood."

"And you're going to pay me?"

"Of course I'm going to pay you."

My cousin was best known for two things: he was a great guide, and he was incredibly cheap. I gave him a questioning look.

"I'll give you a one-eighth share . . . after expenses."

That could be okay. "How many people are you taking on this trip?"

"There's only four people, but—"

"Four people!" I protested. "So you're making practically nothing and offering me a one-eighth share of that?"

"If you'd let me finish my sentence I'd explain. There's only four people going on the trip but they're paying me for all twelve spots."

"Why would they do that?"

"Some people like to have privacy, and they have the money to afford it," Ray explained.

"Wouldn't you figure that going thousands of kilometres up north and then canoeing away into the bush would give you enough privacy?" I asked.

Ray shrugged. "I'm not arguing. Same money for less people means less work."

"They must have more money than brains. Are they Canadian?"

Again Ray shrugged. "Maybe Canadian. Maybe American. Maybe even European or Japanese."

"You don't seem to know much about them."

"All I need to know is that they have money."

"And that's it?"

"If you want to know more, maybe you should radio your father. He's flying them in this morning."

"He is? He's not due back until tomorrow."

"Like I said, these people have money. They paid extra to have him come back here and drop them off before he heads for Cross Lake."

"When will my dad be here?" I asked.

"Less than an hour."

"So, when are you setting out on the trip?" I asked.

"As soon as possible. The supplies are all packed and the canoes are ready to go."

"That changes things," I said.

"What changes things?"

"I'm not going."

"What do you mean you're not going?" Ray demanded.

"I'm not going. At least, I'm not going unless we make a change."

"What sort of change?"

I smiled. "A change in the split. I want more than a one-eighth share."

"I'm not giving you any more! Forget it!"

"Fine. Enjoy your trip," I said. I turned and started to walk away.

"Wait!" Ray practically shouted as he grabbed me by the arm and spun me around. "How much more are you talking about?"

"Not much more. How much do you pay Aylmer?"

"You're not Aylmer!"

"I know. I'm available and I don't have a hangover," I said. "So I think I deserve a quarter share . . . before expenses. Deal?"

Ray didn't answer.

"Better make up your mind. I need to eat and pack . . . so what's it going to be?"

"Quarter share *after* expenses, and you cut all the wood we need for our campfires during the trip," Ray said.

"Quarter share after expenses, I cut all the wood for the campfires, and you help me cut wood for Auntie Francie after we get back."

"Maybe I could get somebody else to come instead of you," Ray said.

"Maybe you could. Of course, the longer you stand here arguing with me the less time you have to find somebody else."

"I should be mad at you."

"No, you shouldn't. You'd do exactly the same thing if you were in my spot, now wouldn't you?"

Ray smiled. "You got yourself a deal." He stuck out his hand and we shook on it.

CHAPTER TWO

I CAUGHT SIGHT OF THE PLANE way off in the distance. It was my father. His plane was bright orange against the brilliant blue of the sky. The colour was a dead giveaway. Nobody else has a paint job like his. My mother did it. She always says that she wants it to be brighter than the sun so it will carry my father through the sky safely.

I also know another reason that she doesn't like to talk about. She wants it that way so it can be seen if the plane ever goes down and needs to be found by the search and rescue team. That's something I try not to think about, but my father always says there are only two types of bush pilots: those who have had an emergency landing and those who haven't had an emergency landing—yet. So far he fits in the second group . . . knock on wood.

The plane took a long slow pass over the far shore of the lake. The wind wasn't strong but it was coming in out of the north. My father had to circle around so the plane would face into it when he landed. The lake was pretty calm. The only time I hate flying is when he has to set it down in the big waves. The only thing worse than being in the plane with him during those landings is not being in the plane and having to watch it from the shore.

I fly with my dad a lot. His busiest time is during the summer when I'm off school and I go with him on lots of trips. Mainly he brings in tourists—people coming to hunt or fish or go on canoe trips—like today. But he also delivers mail and parcels, and he brings in doctors and dentists and police officers who need to get around to different communities. None of the settlements up here are very big, and none are close to any of the others. And of course since there are no roads, the only way in or out is by plane or boat. And really, boats aren't much of an option, especially during the winter.

My father says there's always more business than he can handle. That's good—not just for him, but for me as well. I figure that one day it will be me up there flying my own plane. My plane will be red—just as bright and even easier to see from the sky if it sets down for an emergency landing.

My father made a tight turn and the plane dropped down as he settled in for the final approach across the lake. It seemed to be just skimming across the surface. The pontoons came closer and closer and closer to the water, and then I saw them splash down and plow through, spray and waves being tossed before them as the plane dramatically slowed down. The buzzing of the engine became louder as he taxied it across the water toward the dock. People who have never seen a float plane are always amazed at just how fast it can skim across the water.

I stood up and waved both hands over my head. He always says that seeing me or Mom at the end of the dock waiting for him when he lands is his favourite sight in the world.

"He sure does fly that thing pretty good," Ray said.

"He's the best . . . at least until I start to fly."

"What do you mean *start* to fly," Ray said.

"I mean like really fly . . . by myself."

One of my earliest memories is of being up in that plane. And the first time he let me handle the stick— him right beside me, of course—I couldn't have been more than four years old. My father lets me fly a lot, as long as we're the only ones in the plane.

My father gunned the engines. It takes a lot of power to move the plane through the water. Between the water rudders and engines he was manoeuvring to bring it in right alongside the dock. All at once he cut the engines. The sudden silence always amazes me.

I moved to the end of the dock to greet the plane and catch the first line. The door popped open and my father jumped out onto the pontoon.

"How's it going?" he yelled as the plane continued to glide toward the dock.

"Well . . . good . . . how about for you?"

"Good trip. Is your mother home?"

"She's out in the bush. I don't think she knew you were coming this morning," I said.

"Heck, I didn't even know I was coming till a few hours ago."

He tossed me the line. It bounced out of my hands, and I dropped to my knees and pulled it out of the water. I dragged the plane forward, although my father had taxied it in so perfectly I thought it might have docked itself.

My father, one hand on the side of the plane, made his way down to the other end of the pontoon, grabbed another line and tossed it to Ray. We positioned the plane up against the dock and secured our lines.

My father stepped up onto the dock and gave me a hug. Sometimes I feel like I'm getting a little bit too old to be hugged—at least in front of other people.

"So, Ray," my father said, "I guess they're yours from this point on."

"Mine and Jamie's."

My father gave a questioning look.

"Aylmer isn't feeling good so Jamie's coming with me," Ray explained.

"I hope you negotiated a fair price," my father said.

"Depends on if you mean fair for me or fair for him," Ray said.

My father started to laugh. "Sounds like he did okay for himself."

"Yes, he did," Ray agreed. "And it's time he started earning his money. Why don't you unload the baggage while I meet the customers."

One of the passengers—I guessed the father—had climbed out of the plane and was standing on the pontoon. He looked younger than I had expected. He couldn't have been more than thirty. He also looked fit and athletic. Somehow I figured that anybody with enough money to do all of this would be older, and maybe a little rounder or balding or something. I'd seen enough out-of-shape tourists coming up here for a little wilderness experience. They'd canoe out a day or so and get so exhausted that they'd get stranded out in the bush. More than once they had to arrange to have my father go in and fly them out.

The man jumped onto the dock and a second man came out of the cabin. He looked like a copy of the first—fairly young and athletic looking, though he had fairer hair and was a bit slimmer. They looked like they could be brothers.

"There are kids, right?" I asked.

"Two of them. A boy and a girl," my father said.

Ray went over and introduced himself to the two men. A girl popped out of the plane next. She had sandy blond hair pulled back in a ponytail, and she was quite tall, a bit skinny and looked like her skin hadn't seen a lot of sun. She seemed to be my age. She also seemed a little "green," like the trip hadn't been that enjoyable for her. Lots of people get airsick in small planes, even if they have no problems flying in big ones. Ray went to offer her a hand, but one of the men moved faster and helped her climb out of the plane. A boy—maybe ten or eleven—came out next. The man offered him a hand too but the boy brushed it away and climbed out by himself. He had light brown hair and a heavier build than the girl. He looked to me like a guy who spent more time watching sports on TV than playing them. Ray took the group down the dock and onto the shore, leaving my father and me at the plane.

"Strange-looking family," I commented.

"Not a family," my father said as he undid the latches for the storage compartment.

"What do you mean?"

"The girl and boy are sister and brother, but those two men aren't family."

"I thought that one of them might be the father."

My father shook his head. "Something different going on here."

"How?"

My father hauled out the first pack and handed it to me. "For starters, the way this flight happened. I'm sleeping in my bed when I get woken up and offered a lot of money to change my plans."

"How much money?" I asked.

"Enough that I didn't mind being woken up in the middle of the night and having my flight plans changed," he chuckled.

"Ray said they had lots of money," I said as I took another bag from him. "They booked his whole tour so they could have privacy."

"They had that at the airport, too. I had to taxi down to the far end of the field, away from the terminal, and then this little jet lands and the four of them get out and come straight over to my plane."

"They must have a whole lot of money to afford their own jet," I said.

"Can't be sure it belongs to them. Girl flies pretty nervous. She might have made marks in the arms of the seat she was sitting in, she was gripping it so tight."

"Did she get sick?"

"Nope. Glad she didn't. Hate the smell of puke in my plane. But she was so nervous up there that she almost made me nervous about flying."

"Either way, though, they must have lots and lots of money."

"What they also have are guns."

"I didn't know that this was going to be a hunting trip," I said.

"It isn't. I didn't say they had rifles. I mean guns. Handguns. Both of those men have little shoulder holsters and guns."

"Are you sure?" I asked.

"I spent four hours in a plane with them so I had plenty of time to see, believe me."

"But why would they have handguns?"

"I've also had four hours to think that through. The way I figure it, those two children are the kids of some really rich family, and those two men work for their parents, they're some sort of bodyguards."

"Bodyguards! That's like in a movie or something!"

"Something," my father said, and then he paused. "I don't know. I just wish I knew more about them. I asked lots of questions during our flight, but I didn't get many answers."

"What did you find out?" I asked.

"The girl, Victoria, is your age, thirteen. The boy, Andrew, is eleven, and a bit of a pill. Likes to order people around."

"He ordered *you* around?" I asked in amazement.

My father snorted. "Yeah, right."

My mother always says there are two things that my father doesn't like to do: tell people what to do, and be told what to do.

"The two men are named Nigel and Albert," my father continued.

"Are they Americans?"

"English, at least judging from the way they talk."

My father slammed the hatch shut and we each picked up a couple of bags from the dock. We started off to where Ray's canoes were pulled up on the shore.

"At least the girl was friendly," my father said. "She seemed pretty excited to be going on this trip."

"And the boy . . . Andrew?"

"Spent most of the time on the flight playing with some little computer game he brought with him. That thing nearly drove me crazy with all the sirens and bells and whistles going off," my father grumbled. "So how much time before you and Ray head out?"

"Not long. Grandma's packing me a couple of things and a snack. This all happened pretty fast for me, too. She should be down here soon."

"Well, at least I get to see her for a few minutes before I go," my father said.

"You're leaving that soon?"

"Got to. People are expecting me elsewhere. I'm just going to gas up and go. I'll be back tomorrow. You're gone for five days, right?"

"That's right. You flying them out, too?"

"That's the plan, although I wonder if it'll be sooner than that."

"What do you mean?"

"Think about it. How far do you think two little rich kids are going to paddle before they get tired and want to come back?"

"Judging from their luggage it looks like they've done this before," I said as I gestured down to the packs I was carrying.

"Look closer. Fancy stuff, but it's all brand new. It didn't even come up with them. Somebody delivered it to my plane just before the jet arrived. Here's your grandmother."

I turned around and saw her on the path. She was talking to a couple of my other cousins. On one shoulder she was carrying my beat-up backpack. It certainly didn't compare to the fancy new packs I'd just carted down. Then again, how fancy did it need to be to hold some socks, underwear, a couple of sweaters, and an extra pair of pants?

"You should have radioed in to let us know you were coming this morning," my grandmother said as she approached us.

"I would if I could."

"You're home for a while now, I hope," my grandmother said.

"No such luck. I'm just gassing up and then I have to head out. I've got mail and parcels to deliver to Cross Lake."

"Cross Lake?" my grandmother asked. "Didn't you just pass right over top of the village when you flew up from Edmonton?"

"Almost directly over top of it. I could see the little patch of houses off my port wing as I rounded the lake."

"Then why didn't you stop in?"

"My passengers paid for a direct flight."

"That doesn't make any sense. Fly right past a place and have to take another two-hour flight to get back."

"Money talks."

"Where are these people?" my grandmother asked.

"Ray's with them over by the canoes," I said, pointing them out.

"Come on over and I'll introduce you to them," my father said.

"Always good to meet new people," my grandmother chipped in. "Even if they have more money than brains."

"Grandma!"

"Don't worry, I'm not going to say that to them."

As we walked up, their backs were to us, and they were facing Ray. He was holding a map and explaining to them the route we were going to be taking. We put the bags down and listened as Ray continued to explain things and they asked questions. My father was right, they did have funny English accents. They sounded like they just fell out of a cup of tea. Finally Ray looked up at us.

"I'll introduce you to the rest of our party," Ray said. "You've of course met your pilot, and this is his son, Jamie Ransom. He'll be coming with us."

I reached out my hand and shook everybody else's.

"Are you an Indian too?" the boy asked.

"I'm Cree, northern Cree," I said. "And we like the term Native Canadian a whole lot better."

"Sorry," the girl said with her funny little accent. "My brother didn't mean to offend anybody."

"No offence taken. Just explaining," I said.

"And this lovely lady is Jamie's grandmother and . . . what's wrong?" Ray asked, sounding alarmed.

I turned to my grandmother. Her mouth and eyes were both wide open. She let go of my pack and it fell to the ground at her feet.

"Mom, are you okay?" my father asked.

"Good. Fine. Good," she mumbled.

"These gentlemen are Nigel and Albert, and these two young people are—"

"I know who *they* are," my grandmother said, cutting Ray off.

"You do?" Ray asked.

"Of course," she stammered. "I'm so honoured to meet you both!" She reached out and shook first the girl's hand and then her brother's.

"It's a pleasure," the girl said.

"Yes, a pleasure," the boy echoed.

"This is Victoria," my grandmother said, "and this is Andrew."

"Yes, that's right," Ray said, "but I don't understand how you know them."

"Why wouldn't I know them? This is Princess Victoria, and this young man is Prince Andrew . . . first in line to the British throne."

CHAPTER THREE

IT WAS LIKE ALL AT ONCE nobody knew what to say next. These kids were royalty? That would explain all the money, and maybe the privacy.

"It's such an honour!" my grandmother repeated as she continued to shake the boy's hand, pumping it up and down. She did this little curtsy sort of bow and almost tumbled over. "So honoured! Aren't we honoured?" she said as she turned to the rest of us.

"Um . . . sure . . . yeah," I mumbled.

"You're a prince and princess?" Ray asked.

"Of course they're a prince and princess!" my grandmother exclaimed. "This is Princess Victoria, the oldest daughter of King William, the Princess Royal. She was born on the twenty-fourth of May—the same date as her great-great-great-grandmother, Queen Victoria, whom she's named after. And this," she said, once again making a bowing sort of motion, "is Prince Andrew, oldest son and first in line for the Crown, after his father!"

"Wow, that's impressive," Ray said.

"Very impressive!" my grandmother said. "Royalty!"

"I meant all that stuff you know . . . really impressive."

My grandmother puffed out her chest. "How can we loyal subjects be of service to Your Majesties?"

"Loyal subjects?" I questioned. I was a lot of things, but a loyal subject wasn't one of them.

"We don't want any fuss," the girl—the Princess— answered. "We just want to go on our trip."

"Of course you do," Ray said.

"And we don't want any special treatment," she added.

"You'll be treated like everybody else," Ray assured her. "Of course, we treat everybody like they're the King and Queen of England."

"Thank you, I'm sure we'll have a wonderful time. I can't wait to get started."

"I'm afraid that might not be possible," one of the bodyguards said.

"And why would that be, Albert?" Princess Victoria asked.

"This situation is not good," he said. "We did not anticipate that your identities would be discovered prior to our departure."

"Is there a secure place where we can meet?" asked the other bodyguard, Nigel.

"Secure? You mean like a jail?" my father asked.

"No, a place where we can talk in privacy?"

"Our house," my grandmother said. "I'd be pleased— happy—honoured if the Prince and Princess would come into my house!"

"Thank you, we need to make a decision concerning our options."

"What do you mean, options?" Victoria asked.

"Please, Your Highness. You have to trust me. Now, if you would kindly lead us to the house."

My grandmother led, followed by the bigger of the two guards, the Prince and Princess, the other guard and then Ray and my father and me.

"I thought you had to leave right away," I said to my father.

"I do, but a few extra minutes isn't going to matter. It's not every day you get royalty visiting your house."

By the time we reached the house they were already inside. My grandmother was practically dancing around, and of course she proudly displayed her collection. As she showed off the different pieces, she talked about the history behind each and her knowledge of the Royal Family. It was completely bizarre. Here she was showing them plates and things that had pictures of their relatives on them, and explaining their own family history to them. The girl was pretending to be interested, but the boy looked bored and even a little annoyed.

"And of course so many of my pieces are devoted to your mother, rest her soul," my grandmother said. "That was one of the saddest days of my life. So young— too young. I remember thinking that it wasn't fair that somebody so young and beautiful and loved by so many should be taken from us."

"Yes . . . thank you for your thoughts," Princess Victoria said softly.

Her brother didn't look bored or annoyed any more. His expression was now blank, showing nothing, no emotion.

"And I have to show you this!" She led them to the mantel, reached up and pulled down her framed, autographed picture. She beamed as she handed it to the Princess.

"That's my father and my grandfather," Princess Victoria said.

"That's right," my grandmother said excitedly. "They were here when your daddy was just a boy!"

"I know," she said. "My father has told us many wonderful stories about the adventures he had up here. He wanted us to have the same experience. That's why we're here."

"That's wonderful! Just wonderful! And do you know who was their guide for their trip?" my grandmother asked.

They both shook their heads.

"It was my husband, Jamie's grandfather, who brought your grandfather and father through the bush. And now Jamie's going to be part of bringing the two of you on your adventure!"

"As I said, that's still to be determined," one of the guards pointed out. "There has been a breach in security, and we have to make a decision as to whether or not we are going to cancel this operation."

"This isn't an operation, Albert, this is a vacation," Victoria said.

"A vacation for you is a mission for us, Your Highness," he said. He turned to my father. "If needed, are you free to fly us back to Edmonton?"

"I could . . . if the price was right."

"Hold on, now," Ray said. "We had a deal here, and I expect that I'll still be paid for—"

"You will be paid in full," Nigel said, cutting him off.

"Both of you stop right there!" My grandmother was getting pretty steamed. "We won't be accepting your money for anything! We're just so honoured that you're here with us, and we'd be more than delighted to offer our services in any way possible!"

My father and Ray both stood there, their mouths wide open, speechless.

"Thank you, madam, for your offer, but it is our policy always to pay full dollar and honour all commitments and arrangements," Nigel said.

All at once both my father and Ray started breathing again. They'd known that once my grandmother had made that offer they had no choice but to do what she said. To disagree would have been a slight against her.

"The important thing is the safety of the Prince and Princess," Albert added.

"We *are* safe here!" Princess Victoria exclaimed.

"No, he's right," Prince Andrew said. "Perhaps it would be best if we just flew back and—"

"You're just saying that because you didn't want to come up here in the first place!" she snapped.

"That may be true, but the important issue is our safety. Isn't that correct, Albert?"

"I hardly think that this is a breach of security," the Princess argued. "There are only four people who know we're here, and two of them are coming with us."

"And two are not," her brother observed. "You know what they say, a secret isn't a secret once two people know about it."

"I am most positive we can trust our hosts not to betray our confidence," she said.

My father shrugged. "I won't be telling anybody."

Everybody looked at my grandmother. "I'll be telling everybody!" There was a gasp of disbelief. "Of course, that won't happen until after you're all through with your trip. Then I'll be telling everybody for the rest of my days that I met the future King of England and his sister, a beautiful princess!"

"A decision has to be reached," Albert said.

"A decision was reached," Princess Victoria said. "And that decision was that we should go on a canoe trip. That's what our father wants."

"I think we should go back to Edmonton," her brother said doggedly.

"Are you concerned about the security?" Albert asked in a serious tone.

"No, I heard about this amusement park that's right inside a mall. That would be so cool!"

"If Father had wanted us to go to an amusement park he would have sent us to an amusement park!" she countered. "We are here to go canoeing and that is exactly what we are going to—"

"Both of you be quiet!" Albert snapped.

Everybody—not just the two royals—stopped and stared at him.

"What I mean," he began, "is that it is within my authority to make this decision."

"Could we not just call our father?" Princess Victoria pleaded. "I *know* he would want us to continue."

Albert shook his head. "There are no land lines from here, and radio transmissions are not secure. For better or worse, the decision is mine to make."

"But surely, since it's about us, we need to have input into that decision, and—"

"You have had input," he said, cutting her off. I didn't know you were allowed to cut off a Princess. "I have been your father's security chief for over three years, and in that time he has never, I repeat *never*, questioned my decisions. I know that even if he were standing right here beside us at this very moment, he would agree with whatever decision I make."

Albert's little speech made it quite clear that there wasn't going to be any more discussion from anybody— apparently including Nigel, who I assumed had to be under his command.

"Now, I need to talk to the persons who will be remaining behind," Albert said.

"I've got to get to Cross Lake," my father said, "so this better not take long."

"It will be brief."

"Can I fix us all a little snack, or a cup of tea?" my grandmother asked. "Wouldn't everybody love a cup of tea? I have Earl Grey, isn't that what your grandmother the Queen Mother likes?"

"That's one of her favourites," the Princess answered.

"Thank you, but that won't be necessary at this time," Albert said. He turned and faced the two royal kids. "I'll ask the two of you go elsewhere while we conduct the interviews."

"I can take them down to the canoes, or show them around the village," Ray offered.

"No!" Nigel snapped, suddenly rising to his feet as though he was ready to defend them from Ray. "I mean . . . that would not be wise, to allow them to be exposed to further discovery."

"I could take them to my room," I suggested.

"Is it part of this building?" Albert asked, sounding very anxious.

"Yeah, it's just down there at the end of the hall," I said, pointing at the closed door.

"That would be fine. Thank you."

"Would you mind if *I* go down to the canoes?" Ray asked. "If you decide to go you'll probably want to leave right away, and there are things that need to be done."

"That does sound wise," Albert agreed.

"Good, then I'll just—"

"And Nigel will accompany you. He can offer assistance in any manner you feel is needed."

"Whatever," Ray said. He started for the door and Nigel fell in behind him. There wasn't any question in my mind that Nigel wasn't going along so much to help as to make sure Ray didn't talk to anybody.

"We should go to my room," I said, and I motioned for them to follow me. I opened my bedroom door and instantly regretted my offer. I'd forgotten just how messy I'd left it. It wasn't just that I hadn't made the bed—the dresser top was covered with half-filled glasses and dirty plates, and the floor was littered with clothes I'd kicked off and never bothered to pick up.

I bent down and rolled up a ball of clothing, making sure a dirty pair of underwear was concealed.

"It's a little messy in here," I said as I pitched the clothing across the room and it dropped out of sight behind my bed.

"It's more like a lot messy in here," the Prince said with a laugh.

"Andrew, be polite! It is not that bad!"

"Look around," he said. "You only think it isn't so bad because you're comparing it to *your* room!"

"I do not want you *talking* about my room any more than I want you *in* my room!" she snapped.

As the two of them started to argue I continued to straighten up. I kicked some more clothing under the bed, pushed closed some dresser drawers and closed the door to my cupboard. I started to pull up the covers on my bed and—

"That's a nice computer," Prince Andrew said.

"What?" I asked, even though I'd heard the comment.

"Your computer, it's very nice. Do you have any games?"

"Not a lot. Mostly I use it for my schoolwork and e-mail and—"

"You can get e-mail up here?" the Princess asked.

"Sure, through the satellite. That's how I get my school assignments."

"And if you get e-mail, that means you can go onto the Internet, right?" she asked.

"Of course."

"And go to things like chat rooms."

"I've done that before," I said, although I'd only done it a couple of times. It never made sense to me to spend time talking to a bunch of strangers.

"Could I use your computer to go into a chat room?"

"I guess . . . sure."

"Here we go again!" her brother moaned. "You spend more time talking to people on the computer than you do with real people."

"That's because the people on the computer are more real than some of the people I spend time with. Especially you!"

"Just shut up!" he snapped.

"You shut up, and stay out of my business!"

Did these two always fight like this?

"You can go on my computer," I said, trying to break up the fight.

"Thank you, so much!" she said, sounding sweet again.

I pulled the chair out from the desk. I swept the dirty clothes off with the back of my hand and kicked them out of sight under the desk. Then I sat down and tapped on the keyboard, bringing the computer to life. I moved the cursor over to the Internet icon and the screen popped open. I started to type in my password when I became aware that the Princess was right there, leaning over my shoulder. I stopped.

"Excuse me," I said.

She gave me a puzzled look.

"I have to type in my password. It's personal."

"Oh . . . certainly . . . frightfully sorry," she said, and backed away.

I typed in the remaining three digits, hit Enter and the Internet screen appeared.

"Here it is," I said. "Do you want me to find you the—"

"That's quite all right. I can take care of things," she said. She pushed in close, practically pushing me off the chair.

"I imagine we should feel grateful," her brother said. "When she's chattering away on the Internet, at least she's quiet."

I watched as she flashed from screen to screen. It certainly looked as though she'd had a lot of experience on the computer.

"She's headed to her favourite chat room," he explained. "She likes it so much because some of the kids she talks to are even bigger losers than she is."

"Did I not tell you to shut up, Andrew? Even if my friends are cyber-friends, that still makes them more real than any friends you have."

"I have friends!" he protested.

"You only have people who *pretend* to be your friends because you're royalty!"

"And do you think your friends are any different?" he demanded.

"My cyber-friends don't even know who I am," she argued. "I am anonymous. As far as they're concerned I'm just plain old Torie and nothing special."

"Well, I'll agree with that. You are nothing special," he laughed.

"Be quiet!"

He turned to me. "Some of these kids she talks to don't even have a life. They spend practically every moment of their lives on-line." He turned back to his sister. "Tell Leslie to get a life!"

"You leave poor Leslie alone!"

"Is she on-line now?"

She didn't answer.

"Is she?" he asked again.

"Yes, she is, but don't you go making fun of her. What with her delicate condition and all the trips to the hospital, what else can she do?"

"Yeah, right, and you believe all that. You don't know that she's been sick. You don't even know that she is a she! For all you know, your poor sick Leslie could be a forty-four-year-old man!"

"Even if she were—and she is not—at least she is nice and kind. She has been so interested in everything I have talked to her about, even this trip. Not like some people I know."

"That just shows what a loser she is!"

"I just wish she were here instead of you!"

"Finally we have something we agree about!" he said. "I wish she were here instead of me too!"

"And I wish that for just once in my entire life you would mind your own business and button your lip!"

She turned around and went back to clicking away at the keyboard. The Prince came and sat down beside me on the bed.

"Do you two always argue like that?" I asked.

"Not always. Sometimes we *really* fight."

"More than this?"

"This is nothing! If we all go away on this trip for five days I am certain that you will see much, much worse than this."

"Excuse me!" Princess Victoria called out. "My friend Leslie wants to know if we will be going through rapids. She has always wanted to go through rapids."

"Um . . . I don't really know . . . maybe around some, but we're probably heading east first, and there's none in that direction for a long while."

"Thank you," she said sweetly, and she turned back to the computer.

I didn't know for sure, but I remembered that Ray usually headed that way when he had inexperienced paddlers or small children. The longest stretch of flat water and fewest portages were in that direction.

"Why are you telling her anything, anyway?" Prince Andrew asked. "We're probably not even going."

"We *are* going."

"Don't lie to your little cyber-buddy."

"I'm not lying. I'm just not going to tell her everything that's going on."

My grandmother knocked on the door and came into the room. "Okay, everybody, it's time to go."

"Where are we going?" the Princess asked.

"Yes, where?" her brother echoed.

My grandmother didn't answer right away. Maybe she knew the answer to their question, but I knew that no matter what she said somebody was going to be unhappy.

She smiled. "You're going out into the bush!"

Victoria cheered as her brother cursed under his breath. She turned back to the keyboard and tapped out a final goodbye to Leslie.

CHAPTER FOUR

MY FATHER TAXIED THE PLANE AWAY from the dock and out to open water. I watched as he opened up the engines and it started to pick up speed. My father is a great pilot, but even for great pilots, take-offs and landings are the most dangerous. And a float plane faces a whole other set of hazards. On a regular runway the surface doesn't move, or have objects hidden just beneath the surface. A big rogue wave or a hidden log could rip open a pontoon or even flip a plane right over.

The plane lifted off and I offered a silent "thank you." He circled around, gaining height. Then he waggled the wings to say goodbye and broke off toward his destination.

"That is a very exciting job."

I turned around. It was the Princess. That was such a strange thought. This girl with the brown hair, freckles and teeth that seemed just a little bit too white . . . was a princess!

"And I imagine it's dangerous," she added.

"It's not that bad." I never like to admit it's danger-ous. "I don't even know anybody who's even been hurt in a plane crash."

She suddenly looked down at the ground and I was hit in the head by something I suddenly remembered. Her mother—their mother—was dead. She'd died in an airplane accident a few years ago. How stupid could I be?

"I'm . . . I'm sorry," I mumbled. "I didn't mean anything."

"I know," she said softly. "It's all right. It was a long time ago."

I racked my brain trying to remember just how long ago it was. I remembered how upset my grandmother had been and how she'd cried for the better part of two days. And I even recalled seeing part of the funeral on TV. There really hadn't been that much choice because it had been on half the channels our satellite brought in, and then parts of it were on every news broadcast. It had to be three years ago.

"Do you worry about something happening to your father?" she asked.

"No . . . not a lot . . . sometimes," I mumbled, still struggling for words.

"I worry a great deal about mine."

"Does he fly?" I asked.

She laughed. It was a nice laugh. "He doesn't fly the planes but he certainly travels in them a great deal. Of course, that's not what I find so worrisome."

"What is?"

She motioned to where Albert and Nigel stood beside Ray.

"It is a rather strange existence to need to have

specially trained bodyguards carrying weapons to protect you everywhere you go, all the time."

"I guess it would be. At least up here it shouldn't be such a big problem," I said.

"That's what my father said."

"Jamie!" Ray called out, and I turned around. "Come on over here, and bring the young lady with you!"

We walked over to the canoes, where Ray already stood with Prince Andrew and the two bodyguards.

"Before we get started I want to know just how much paddling experience my guests have," Ray said.

"I have canoed a great deal," Princess Victoria said.

"And you?" he asked her brother.

"A few times. Frankly I didn't like it very much."

"And the two of you?" Ray asked Albert and Nigel.

"We have received instruction in orienteering in addition to our survival training. We are very qualified," Albert said.

"Either of you ever been in the bush before?"

"Not technically."

"But we both know how to paddle a canoe," Nigel said.

Ray slowly shook his head. "I guess that pretty well decides how we're going to pair up. The little guy goes with me and Jamie will share with the girl and—"

"I'm sorry, but that's not possible," Albert said, cutting him off.

"What's not possible?" Ray asked.

"It is not possible to have the Prince and Princess separated from us. One of us *must* be with them at *all* times."

"You're not going to be separated," Ray said. "The two of you are just going to be in another canoe. We're all taking the same piece of water to the same place, you know."

"We must be right with them. I am in charge of their security."

Ray didn't say anything right away, but I could tell from his expression that he was thinking. He bent down slowly and picked up his pack from the canoe.

"Then I hope you all enjoy your trip. Leave the canoes right here when you're done. Come on, Jamie," he said, and he started to walk away.

"Excuse me!" Albert practically yelled. Ray stopped and turned back around. "You can't just leave!"

"Why not?" Ray asked. "You already told me that you were in charge, that you're in charge of security, so why do you need me?"

"You're the expert! You're the leader!" Albert exclaimed.

Ray smiled and took a few steps back. He dropped his pack back in the canoe. "Now that that's understood, let me explain things a little. You two may be in charge of *their* security," he said, pointing at the Prince and Princess, "but out here I'm in charge of *everybody's* security. Understand?"

Albert and Nigel reluctantly nodded in agreement.

"And while you may be a prince," he said, pointing at Andrew, "and you a princess," he said, nodding at Victoria, "out here I'm the *king*. And Jamie here is the *vice-king*."

"Vice-king?" Prince Andrew asked. "What is a vice-king?"

"The guy who tells everybody what to do when the king isn't around," Ray explained. "And if those terms aren't good enough, then we just aren't going. Because you know I'd be just as happy to spend the next five days fishing by myself."

Everybody looked at Albert.

"Please," Princess Victoria pleaded. "We'll stay close together. Besides, wouldn't we be safer if we were right there with the people who know the bush the best?"

"She's got a point," Ray said. "Any danger you're going to meet up here is going to be from something that me and Jamie are more experienced with and able to deal with."

What sort of danger did he mean? There wasn't much that was very dangerous up here . . . at least if you knew what you were doing.

Albert looked at the Princess, then the Prince, and finally at Ray. "I imagine that will be sufficient for our security requirements."

"So the pairings are going to be like I said," Ray continued. "I'm with . . . with . . . what are we supposed to call you two?"

"My friends call me Victoria, or sometimes Vicky."

"Not Torie?" I asked.

"Never!" she scoffed.

"But on the computer—"

As soon as I said that, Victoria gave me a look that would have stopped a herd of elephants. Just then it was easy to believe she was royalty. In any case, I was obedient and shut up right away.

"And him?"

"Andrew would do fine," he said.

"Sounds about right," Ray agreed. "So, Vicky, you're with Jamie, and I'll take Andrew with me."

Ray had everything already set up and we quickly settled into the canoes. My grandmother came down to say goodbye, and when she heard me call the Princess "Victoria" her mouth dropped open so wide I thought her jaw was going to hit the ground. Just for kicks I called her that a couple more times and added an "Andrew."

We headed off to the east—the way I'd figured we'd go. Ray took the lead, I followed, and the two security guys came up last. It was pretty clear pretty fast that there were really only two of us that knew what we were doing. Ray wasn't setting any speed records, and it was easy for me to stay right with him. Albert and Nigel struggled to keep up. They both looked like they were plenty strong, but neither really had much technique going for them.

From my perch at the stern of the canoe the biggest part of my view was the back of the Princess. She was working very hard, digging in the paddle and trying to hold up her end. It looked like she knew the way she was supposed to paddle but wasn't very good at doing what she was supposed to do. We moved along with almost no conversation. It would have been nice to talk a little. On her part, most of her breath was going toward working the paddle. For me, I just didn't know what to say. I didn't know that many girls, and I really didn't know that many girls my age. Especially ones who weren't related to me. Besides, what do you talk to a princess about? Should I ask what TV shows she watched or how she liked school—did she even go to school? Probably she just did princess things. Things like going to fancy parties, or riding around in carriages, or having people do her hair, or maybe having tea, or playing polo. Polo looked like it might be fun. Not that I'd ever been on a horse, but I'd seen them a couple of times.

"You are very lucky," she said, turning around.

I felt embarrassed because I'd been looking right at her when she turned. But where else was I supposed to be looking?

"Lucky?"

"You get to live up here all the time."

"I guess that's lucky."

"It is. To have so much space and so few people would be such a joyous circumstance."

"Um . . . sure." She sure did talk funny. It wasn't just the accent, but the strange way she put words together— *joyous circumstance*—what the heck did she mean by that? Was she trying to sound fun, or cool, or good, or what?

"My father recalls his trip here as one of the very best times of his life," she continued. "Getting away from everything and everybody and all the expectations and responsibilities."

"Responsibilities?" I asked.

"Hundreds and hundreds of them. Our time is so scheduled that we hardly have a moment for ourselves. It isn't like I spend all my time going to parties and playing polo."

For a split second I was taken aback. Thank goodness I hadn't said any of the things I'd been thinking.

"And at every event I must meet with people. Sometimes literally hundreds of people. And even if I am not directly meeting with these individuals, there are still hundreds or even thousands of people who are constantly observing me. At times I feel like I am some sort of exhibit at the zoo."

"That would be different," I said.

"It would be different for me to be in a position where my every comment, sneeze and gesture were not seen, photographed, interpreted and then written up in newspapers around the globe! Do you have any idea how unsettling that becomes? I'm constantly being observed. Do you have any idea what that feels like?"

"Sort of."

"You do?"

"Not the written-about or taking-pictures part, but I understand about being watched. Try living in a village of two hundred people where everybody not only knows everybody but is related to you one way or another. I can't even sneeze without everybody asking me if I'm coming down with a cold."

She laughed. "Exactly. The worst part for me, though, is the smiling."

"Smiling?"

"Yes, smiling and waving. I'm expected to be perpetually happy, friendly and polite no matter how nasty or rude the people I'm dealing with are being."

"That would be hard," I admitted.

"Sometimes I'd like to just tell them to take a flying leap!"

"Why don't you?" I asked.

"Because the next day it would reported in every newspaper in the world: 'Princess Victoria is *royally spoiled*,' or something like that."

"With me it's just everybody in the village. I guess that would be difficult."

"Believe me, it is. That was perhaps the biggest reason I was looking forward to coming here. I simply wanted to be left alone, to be away from the spotlight."

"It's okay if you don't want to talk," I said.

"No, no, I'm enjoying our talk. I'm enjoying all of this."

"Um . . . it sounds like your brother doesn't feel the same way. He doesn't seem to like the idea of being up here."

"My brother does not exactly like any idea. He's quite the little pain, you know. Do you have any little brothers?"

"Nope, just me."

"Lucky you. The only thing worse than having a little brother is having a little brother who is going to be the king of England some day. He can be such a little brat, and everybody lets him get away with it. Sometimes he angers me so much, I want to throttle him."

"Do you mean like smack him around?" I asked, not entirely sure what she meant by "throttle."

"Oh, I would truly like to give him a good slap."

"Hit him upside his head."

"I'd love to do that, just once," she said gleefully.

"You mean you've never hit him, not even once?" I asked in disbelief. They'd looked like they were going to come to blows a couple of times already.

"I cannot very well hit the first in line to the throne, now can I?" she asked.

"Why not? You're a princess. If anybody should be able to take a shot at him it should be you."

She laughed. "I enjoy the way your mind works."

"Thanks, I guess."

"He might like this experience more if he understood what an adventure this will be. Unfortunately he just does not know about the north the way I do."

"I didn't know you'd been up here before."

"Well, I haven't. But I have read books, and seen movies and researched websites and heard stories and everything!"

"But you've never been up in the bush?"

"Not really the bush, but I have been in *northern* England. We have a large estate in the north. It's pretty remote. In places there are no towns for dozens and dozens of kilometres."

I tried to contain it but a laugh popped out. She looked hurt. I hadn't meant to hurt her feelings.

"It's okay, I don't know anything about cities. The biggest place I've ever been is Edmonton, and it scared me."

"Are you implying that I am afraid of the bush?" she asked indignantly.

"I'm not implying anything. I know that I'm nervous in cities and—"

"You said 'scared.' That is significantly worse than simply being a little nervous," she snapped.

"Either way, anybody who doesn't know the bush would be plain *stupid* not to be really, really scared."

"I'm neither stupid nor scared. I have sufficient information and knowledge to get us through any situation that we might confront. In fact, if you have any questions, please do not feel uncomfortable asking for *my* assistance."

"*Me,* ask *you* for help?" I asked indignantly. "Just who do you—?"

"Hey, you want to keep it down?" Ray yelled over. "It's supposed to be peaceful up here!"

"Sorry," I called back.

"Yes, terribly sorry," she added, though I wasn't sure she really meant it.

"Let's just keep paddling," I said.

"Certainly," she said. "Would you mind if I asked you a question?"

"Nope, go ahead, shoot."

"Your name . . . it doesn't sound very Native."

"My mother always liked the name Jamie, and—"

"No, I meant your last name, Ransom," she said, cutting me off.

"I know lots of Natives with that last name." Of course, in my village about half the people had that last name. "What were you expecting me to be called, Golden Eagle Song or Naked Bear or something like that?"

"Not exactly . . . well . . . possibly."

"Maybe with some tribal groups, but not ours. Closest you're going to get is Ray. You can pretend it's short for *Ray of Sunlight* instead of Raymond, if that'll help you feel like you've met a real-life Indian."

"I really meant no offence," she pleaded.

I held my tongue. "I guess there's none taken . . . at least not this time. Let's just paddle."

CHAPTER FIVE

RAY ANGLED HIS CANOE toward a spot on the shore where I'd camped before. It was a good site with a sandy beach and enough open space to set up our tents. I knew that he would normally have travelled farther than this, but it was probably wise to call it a day. It had been obvious to me for a while that our guests weren't doing so well. Andrew had pretty well stopped paddling, and Victoria's strokes had gotten awfully short and choppy. I had to hand it to her, though, she must have been really tired but she hadn't stopped trying to do her share of the work.

Way back, Albert and Nigel were struggling not to fall any farther behind. They both looked to be pretty strong guys, certainly stronger than me, but canoeing isn't so much about strength as it is technique—the sort of thing you get from experience and doing instead of taking a course.

"Looks like we're putting in," I noted.

"For the night or for a portage?"

"No portage here, so it must be for the night."

"That's wonderful," she gushed.

"You tired?"

"I could go on if I had to." She paused. "How far do you think we've gone?"

"Hard to say for sure."

"Could you make an educated guess?"

"Well . . . we canoed for about four hours before we stopped for lunch, so we probably did around twelve kilometres and—"

"Didn't we cover more than that?" she asked.

I shook my head. "And then we did about the same . . . maybe a little more . . . between lunch and now."

"So you think we've only done twenty-four or twenty-five kilometres?"

"I think so."

"You must be wrong. Surely we travelled farther."

I shrugged. "Could have."

"My father told us about days when he canoed almost double that distance."

"That's possible. It was a short day today, and we weren't moving very quickly."

"I thought we were keeping up a good pace," she said.

"Pretty good for city people. Besides, your father was with my grandfather, right?"

"That's what your grandmother said."

"Then that would explain them travelling a lot farther. When my grandfather went out for what he called 'a little paddle' he dipped his paddle in the water and didn't stop. He was amazing! I went out with him on a trip when I was about five and he was in his seventies. We covered over two hundred kilometres in five days, and you know that I didn't contribute much to the paddling."

"Probably as much as my brother did today," she said.

"Well . . . maybe a little bit more than that."

She burst out laughing. She really did have a nice laugh.

"Did you spend much time with your grandfather?"

"It's hard not to when you live in the same little village."

"When did he pass on?" she asked.

"Just a while ago."

"You must miss him."

Of course I missed him. He was my grandfather. I nodded.

"I didn't get to know my grandfather very well," she said. "He died when I was very little."

"If you want to know anything about *your* grandfather you should ask *my* grandmother," I said.

She laughed again. "She certainly did take us by surprise when she recognized us, and then, when she began reciting our family history . . . and all those plates and pictures and mementos! It was so, so . . ."

"Strange?" I asked.

"Well, I was thinking 'sweet,' but if one was to ever think about it, there certainly is something unusual about finding pictures of your family in the house of somebody you have never met before."

"There are actually more pictures of *your* family in my house than there are of *my* family."

Again she laughed.

"But I guess it wouldn't have been so sweet if it had cost you the trip," I noted.

"That would have be so unfortunate . . . a tragedy."

Up ahead Ray and Andrew had already made land. Ray had pulled the canoe up onto the shore and was pulling out the packs. Andrew was off to the side, sitting on a rock.

"I'll bring us in close, then I'll jump out and pull you into shore so you won't get wet," I said.

"I'll do that," Victoria said.

"That's okay, I can do it."

"And so can I. I believe that proper canoe etiquette calls for the person in the bow to leave the craft and bring the canoe in."

"I don't know nothing about etiquette, but if you want to jump in and get wet instead of me, then I'm not going to argue."

I changed course so the canoe was coming straight in for the sandy beach. Suddenly she shifted around and threw her legs over the side, swung herself over and dropped into water up to her waist. Why hadn't she waited until we got closer to shore? She waded through the water, dragging the canoe behind her, and pulled the bow up onto the beach. I stood up and carefully walked up the canoe and jumped out onto the shore. Hey, any landing that ended with my feet dry was a good one! I grabbed the bow of the canoe and, along with Victoria, pulled it up and completely out of the water.

"Jamie, why didn't you bring the canoe in instead of—?"

"He wanted to!" Victoria called out, cutting Ray off. "But I wouldn't hear of it!"

"I guess he couldn't force you to let him, but if you're going to be doing that again you might want to wait until you actually get close to the shore," Ray pointed out.

"I think I will be able to remember that lesson."

"Good. So how did you enjoy your first day on the water?"

"I really liked it," she said.

"Tired?"

She nodded.

"Well, there's not much more for you to do for the rest of the night. Just grab your pack and bring it up by your brother, and then we'll get everything set up."

She took her pack and started up the slope to where Andrew sat.

"How was she?" Ray asked quietly.

"She did okay. She'll learn to paddle better as we—"

"I didn't mean about her paddling. What was she like?"

"Fine. Friendly. Talked."

"You mean she didn't complain about the bugs, and how hard the seat was, and how she didn't want to be here and how hot it was?"

"No, nothing like that."

"Then you got the better half of the pair."

"Was he that bad?"

"Worse. If those bodyguard fellas hadn't been in the canoe right behind me I would have hit him with the paddle just to get him to shut up."

"Do you want me to take him tomorrow?" I asked, regretting the words as I spoke them.

Ray shook his head. "Can't do that. Kid hardly paddled a lick the whole way so it's best he stays with me. Worst part was those ears of his."

"His ears?"

"Didn't you notice them?"

"Not really," I said, although thinking it through I did think they were on the large side.

"They're *huge!*" Ray exclaimed. "Him sitting in front of me like that in the canoe those ears blocked my view, and I swear when he turned his head the wrong way they caught the breeze and practically turned us around!"

I burst out laughing. Victoria and Andrew both turned around and stared down at us from the campsite. They were probably wondering what I found so funny. I'd have to think something up in case one of them asked later.

"I figure if I could only get him facing the right way with the wind behind us, those ears could work like sails and neither one of us would need to paddle!"

"Then maybe he *should* be in my canoe," I said.

"I can't do that to my little cousin. I'm stuck with him. Simple as that."

"Probably best."

"But do me a favour, you take Prince Charming with you when you gather wood for the fire. With any luck you might lose him."

I grabbed my pack and brought it up from the canoe. Victoria and Andrew sat silently. Neither looked like they had much energy left.

"Time to get moving," Ray said.

"Moving? You mean we're getting back into the canoes?" Andrew asked.

"Moving your legs. Andrew, you go with Jamie and gather firewood."

"I am *far* too tired," he said.

"And you're going to be *far* too cold and hungry without a fire," Ray said.

"I can go," Victoria volunteered.

"Nope," Ray said. "Setting up here at the camp is harder work than gathering firewood and I need the stronger of the two of you here."

"Couldn't Jamie just go by himself?" Andrew asked.

"Nobody goes anywhere by themselves up here. Not smart."

"Perhaps I could have Nigel or Albert go?" Andrew suggested.

Ray walked over until he was practically standing on top of Andrew. "Your bodyguards aren't here right now, so I think that maybe, if you're smart, you'll do what I tell you to do. Understand?"

Andrew practically jumped to his feet. I guess he wasn't used to people talking to him like that.

I started off into the bush. Reluctantly, Andrew followed behind me. We'd hardly lost sight of the campsite—and Ray—when he sat down again on a rock. I walked back to him, carrying the first few small pieces of wood that I'd picked up.

"Do you know why we never go out anywhere by ourselves?" I asked.

He didn't answer.

"Bears."

"Bears?" It sounded like I'd got his attention.

"Mainly blacks, but some grizzlies as well."

Andrew looked slowly around like he was expecting to see one.

"This is bear country. I've hardly ever gone on a trip without seeing some bears. Do you know the difference between the two types?" I asked.

"The colour, I would imagine," he said.

"Of course the colour and the size, but the biggest difference is in the attitude."

I started walking again and he jumped up and came after me. "What do you mean?"

I bent down and picked up a piece of wood. "Here, take this."

"What do you mean, the attitude?" he repeated as he took the wood from me.

"Okay, let's say we're out here gathering firewood—"

"Wouldn't it be safer if we were back at the camp instead of in the woods?" he asked, cutting me off.

"Not at all. The camp is where the food is. Food attracts bears. We're actually safer out here. Do you want me to continue?"

He nodded.

"So we're gathering wood and we run into a black bear. Do you know what it's most likely to do?"

"Kill us?" he asked, nervously.

"It could, but if he has a choice, most likely he's just going to turn and get away from us. He may be three or four times as big as us, but he's pretty shy, and he thinks we're pretty scary."

"Us?"

"Some of us more than others. The black will only charge if it sees you as a threat to itself or its young, or if you surprise it."

"How do you surprise it?"

"Can you get that piece of wood over there?" I said pointing off to the side.

He grabbed it.

"You surprise a bear when it doesn't hear you coming and you practically bump into it."

"So should we make more noise?" he asked.

"I don't think we could make any more noise. Problem is, if you make too much noise you can chase away the black bears, but you might just attract the grizzlies."

He shut his mouth and stopped dead in his tracks.

"Here, take these," I said, and I passed over half of the wood I'd been gathering. I started walking again and he practically bumped into me in his rush to be right by my side.

"Now, the grizzly is way different from his cousin bear. Besides being up to three times as big, it's what's going on in his head."

"What's going on?"

"He's not shy and he's not scared. Not of us or of anything. When he sees us, he's only thinking one thing."

"What's that?"

"He's thinking, '*When was the last time I ate?*'"

Andrew stopped walking once again. "You're making a joke . . . right?"

"No. Grizzlies will eat just about anything they can catch, and they're amazingly fast for something that big."

"Are they faster than a person . . . faster than me?" Andrew asked.

"A lot faster than you. But I'm not worried."

"You're not?"

"'Course not."

"Because you're faster than a grizzly?" he asked.

"I don't have to be."

"You don't?" he asked.

"Nope. He probably can't catch two of us. I'll be okay as long as I can outrun *you*."

Andrew looked shocked.

"Now stay close and let's get the rest of the wood." I turned and walked away, struggling to keep the smile off my face.

The three tents were already set up when we arrived back. I dumped my wood in a heap beside a stone-ringed firepit. Andrew dropped his down on top of my pile. I started to break up the smaller pieces and pile them into a little teepee. Next I ripped up some bark and put it around the teepee. Finally I put a few bigger pieces around, stacking them up.

"I am curious to see how you are going to start the fire," Victoria said.

I turned around. She was standing right behind me.

"How do you think I'm going to start the fire?" I asked.

"I wasn't sure. Perhaps rubbing sticks together, or a special Native tool, or—"

"Oh, I have one of those special Native tools," I said cutting her off. I reached into my pocket and pulled out a pack of matches and held them up to her.

"We call them *matches*." I pulled one out, closed the cover, struck it on the back and dropped it into the firepit. It caught easily, and a little fire started to grow.

CHAPTER SIX

I HEARD A TWIG SNAP just outside the tent. All that talk about bears hadn't made just Andrew nervous. Most of what I'd told him was actually true.

Ray slept peacefully, if not silently, beside me. If I was going to wake him up to ask him about the noise, I'd better pray there actually was a bear outside. Waking Ray up wasn't pretty.

Silently I shifted out of my sleeping bag and crawled to the flap. Outside, the fire continued to burn, creating a small island of light in the darkness. Just at the edge I caught sight of the silhouette of a figure sitting motionless on a rock. It looked small. Was it Andrew, or Victoria? If it was Andrew, did I really want to spend any more time with him? But if it was Victoria . . .

Slowly, so as not to make any sound, I undid the zipper of the tent. I slipped out through the opening and zipped it back up. Ray was still undisturbed. Quietly I walked away from the tent toward the lone figure sitting by the fire. It was Victoria!

"Hi," I said.

She jumped to her feet and spun around. "Do you always sneak up on people like that?" she demanded.

"Sorry, I didn't mean to scare you."

She took a deep breath and let out a loud sigh. "I imagine I am perhaps a trifle jumpy. Haven't you been able to sleep either?"

"I was sleeping okay. I heard some noise . . . out here by the fire."

"I am frightfully sorry if I disturbed you."

"It could have been anything," I said. "I'm surprised you're up, though. I thought after all that paddling you'd be dead tired."

"I must admit, I'd assumed the same thing," she admitted. "At first I believed I was having trouble falling asleep because it was still light out."

"That does take some getting used to," I said. "End of June, we only have about an hour when the sun is completely down and it's really dark."

"That would be amazing."

"Of course in December we get the same thing in reverse, barely any light."

"Well, even when it got dark tonight I still wasn't able to sleep. I thought I would come out here and look at the stars."

My gaze followed the little bits of burning ash and embers up into the sky. The smoke from the fire was helping to keep the mosquitoes away. There was a slim slice of moon directly overhead, surrounded by thousands of stars.

"I am not accustomed to seeing such an array of stars," she said.

"You don't go out at night very often?" I asked.

"There are simply no stars to see. Only a few are visible—the North Star, sometimes the rest of the Big Dipper, perhaps a dozen or so more."

"How's that possible?" I asked. "We'd both be looking up at the same sky."

"Same sky, but where I usually stand the sky is obscured by pollution."

"There's that much smoke?"

"There is a great deal of smoke and smog, but it is mainly *light* pollution that is the culprit."

"Wouldn't *heavy* pollution be a bigger problem?" I asked.

She laughed slightly and then stopped herself. "No, no, I am referring to the effects caused by all the artificial lights in a city area. Things like car headlights, streetlights, lights from houses, businesses and offices. They act to create a haze that hides all but the brightest stars," she explained.

"Sort of like how the stars are up in the sky during the day but the sun's light blocks them out," I said.

"Exactly. It is never truly dark in a city, even in the middle of the night. Not like it is here. Away from this fire it's pitch-black. I've been staring out into the surrounding forest. It is a wonder how little I can actually see."

We sat in silence. The only sound was the crackling of the fire. I got up and threw on a couple more pieces of wood. A cascade of flickering ash rose skyward.

"You are very fortunate to live in such a place," she said.

"I hadn't really thought much about it until this last year."

She gave me a questioning look.

"I was away at school," I explained.

"There is no school in your village?"

"There is for the little kids, but once you hit grade seven you have to head south if you want to keep going."

"You went to Edmonton?"

"I didn't say way down south. Just to Fort McMurray. That's about a two-hour flight from here."

"And did your father fly you in every day?"

"I wish. I lived down there. There are dormitories. It's a residential school."

"Did you come home for weekends?"

"I did sometimes because my father could fly me in, but for most kids it's often months before they get to go home. Some can't even go home for Christmas."

"That is so unfortunate, but I imagine there is no alternative."

I shrugged. "Some kids just quit school."

"You mean they don't finish the higher forms?"

"Do you mean grades?"

She nodded.

"Some drop out partway through grade seven. They just go home and don't come back."

There were times I'd been tempted myself—to stay home and forget about school, pick up work in the village like some kids did and never leave. But my family would have killed me! And anyway, I had other plans. Big plans.

"But surely they must realize that their education is essential to pursue higher learning and professional status."

"What?" I asked.

She didn't answer right away. "To go to university and get a good job, you need to go to school."

"University isn't for everybody, and lots of jobs don't take much schooling. Ray's only got grade seven and he has a pretty good business. Trappers don't need any education. My mother's only got grade ten and her art sells really well."

"I was not intending to slight anybody," she said.

"You just don't know how hard it is to be away from your family like that," I said.

"I do know."

"I don't mean like on a vacation for a few days."

"I know *exactly* what you mean," she said. "I also attend a residential school."

"You?"

"For the past three school years, since I was ten years old."

"But you live in a city. There must be schools around."

"Many. Dozens. Perhaps hundreds."

"So why don't you go to one of those?" I asked.

"It's tradition."

"What does that mean?"

"My mother and my grandmother and her mother before that all attended the same institution."

"Institution? I thought we were talking about schools."

She laughed. "Apparently they're the same thing."

"And what about your brother?"

"He will be leaving home for the first time this fall."

"At least you'll have some family around then," I said.

"My school is exclusively a girls' school, and he'll be attending a boys' academy in Scotland."

"Is your school in Scotland?"

"England."

"So you two won't even be in the same *country*?"

She smiled. "Now that you have become acquainted with my brother, you can surely appreciate the benefits of that arrangement."

We both laughed.

"You are going to continue your education, aren't you?"

"I don't have a choice. I want to be a pilot."

"Like your father."

"Exactly. How about you? What do you want to be when you. . . ?" I let the sentence trail off as I suddenly realized who I was talking to. "I guess you'll be a queen."

"Actually, I'll still be a princess. The crown passes to the firstborn male. Women get to be queen only if there are no boys in the direct line of descent. My brother's wife—assuming he finds somebody daft enough to wed him—will become the queen."

"That doesn't seem fair," I said. I was thinking that she might make a pretty great queen, and that Andrew was likely to be a royal pain in the neck once he really got a chance to throw his weight around. "Doesn't it bother you that your little brother is going to get the top job?"

"Honestly? No. Being the monarch is not an easy life. Ask my father if you don't believe me. It's a tremendous responsibility, and it comes with a lot of hard work. Not to mention the endless public appearances and visits from heads of state. What I'm hoping to be is a princess with a degree in medicine."

"A doctor?"

"A pediatrician, to be exact. I want to work with children."

"That's a good thing to do. There's always kids, and they do seem to get sick a lot."

"But I wouldn't want to work in a big city. The cities already have enough doctors and hospitals. I'd like to work in an area that does not have many resources."

"Like up here?" I asked. "There aren't many doctors here."

"I imagine this is exactly the sort of place I am thinking of."

"My dad flies patients out and doctors in all the time," I said.

"The helping part appeals to me, but I am not sure I could handle the flying."

"Lots of people don't like flying," I said reassuringly.

"Did your father tell you how scared I was when we flew in?" she asked nervously.

"Not really," I lied. "Was it hard for you?"

She nodded. "Afraid so. I'm already dreading the flight out."

"My father's really a great pilot," I said.

"I am sure he is," she said. "And I am equally sure you will be, too."

"Thanks. I can already fly."

"You can?"

"My dad lets me take the stick all the time. He says I'm a natural."

She didn't say anything, and once again we sat in silence. Maybe I shouldn't have mentioned the plane—it had to be hard for her to be reminded of her mother's death all the time.

"Sometimes people outgrow their fears," she said softly. "Perhaps one day you will be flying me into those communities."

"I could do that," I said, and then I turned so I was facing her directly. "I bet you're going to be as good a doctor as I'm going to be a pilot."

"Thank you, Jamie, it's sweet of you to say so. . . ."

CHAPTER SEVEN

THE BRIGHT SUN FILTERED through the material of the tent. I sat up. What time was it? Ray was already gone. I pulled myself out of my sleeping bag and started to crawl out of the tent when Ray—or at least his legs—appeared at the opening. He bent down, and in each hand he held a steaming cup.

"Good *afternoon*," he said. "About time you got up."

"What time is it?"

"Almost seven. Coffee?" He offered me one of the cups.

"Thanks." I took a sip. It was good and hot. "I didn't mean to sleep in."

"That's okay. It's not like anybody else is up yet."

"They're all still asleep?"

"Not surprising. Fresh air and lots of exercise can really tire a person out." He paused. "And sitting up half the night by the fire talking doesn't help either."

"Did we wake you up?"

"I heard you two. Did you have a nice little chat?"

"I guess so."

"Guess?" he asked, sarcastically. "Weren't you there?"

"Of course. It *was* a nice chat."

"How old is that little princess?" Ray asked.

"Thirteen. The same as me."

"That's what I thought. You two are getting along real good," Ray said with a smirk. "*Real* good."

"I always get along with people," I said. "Is there anything wrong with that?"

"Nothing, nothing at all." He paused. "I just think it's all so . . . so . . . sweet."

"Sweet?"

"Yeah, sweet. I just have one question."

"And that is?"

"If you and the Princess got married, would I have to call you Your Highness, or Your Majesty or King Jamie or—"

"Actually, it would be Prince Jamie."

We turned around. It was Albert. Nigel stood just behind him and off to the side.

"A male who marries into the royal bloodline can never be king."

"He was just joking around!" I protested.

"Since a king outranks a queen, it would not be possible for an outsider—somebody who has merely married into the family—to be the actual head of state. Thus, the highest rank you could ever acquire would be that of prince."

"That's too bad, Jamie," Ray said. "I think King Jamie has a real ring to it."

I wanted to tell him to shut up, but I knew that would only encourage him to keep going.

"So that would make him your boss, right?" Ray asked Albert.

"And yours as well, technically, since Canada is a constitutional monarchy. Though your laws are governed by your constitution, Britain's king is your formal head of state, and all Canadian citizens are loyal subjects of the Crown."

"That'll be the day when I take orders from any king," Ray said.

"Actually," Albert said, "I was hoping to speak to you about that."

"About what?" Ray set his jaw and put his hands on his hips, like he was ready for an argument.

"The Prince spoke to me last night," Albert said.

"He does a lot of talking, doesn't he?" Ray observed.

"He mentioned that he felt that you had been, how can I say this, rather rough with him prior to our canoe landing."

"I just told him to gather some wood," Ray snapped.

"And he also said that while he was out with Jamie collecting the wood that you threatened to throw him to a grizzly bear," Albert added, looking directly at me.

"I didn't say that!" I protested. After all, I'd only said that I'd let one eat him if it was chasing the two of us.

"So what's your point?" Ray said loudly.

"Please keep your voice down. I would prefer that our conversation remain private, and—"

"I don't care what you want. I'll treat him, and *you,* the way that—"

"Please, there is no need to be angry," Albert said.

"You think you can tell me how to behave and I don't have the right to be angry?" Ray demanded.

"No, you don't understand," Albert said.

"I understand pretty darn good!"

"No, you don't. I wanted you to know that I . . . we . . . the Prince's father and I, hope that you will continue to treat him as you did last night."

"Nobody is going to tell me I have to take guff from any snot-nosed little brat just because—" Ray suddenly stopped. "What did you just say?"

"It is the opinion of the Prince's father that his son has become very much a *little snot-nosed brat*."

"He said that?" I asked.

"Not those words exactly, but it is rather obvious to anyone who has spent more than a few moments in Andrew's presence," Albert said.

"His father is of the belief," Nigel added, "that this trip—being forced to work and fend for himself—will help to mature his son. Perhaps have a positive influence on his behaviour and attitude."

"So, you *don't* want me to take it easy on him?" Ray asked.

"Not in the least. Make him be responsible, drive him to do what's expected of him. We ask only two things," Albert said.

"And they are?"

"Please don't put him in positions that could expose him to physical danger beyond the normal expectations of this trip," Nigel said.

"And the second thing?"

"No matter how tempting it may be, refrain from clocking him," Albert said.

"Clocking him?"

"I think it means like throttling him," I said. "You know, smacking him."

"Regardless of how obnoxious he becomes."

"I've never hit one of my customers," Ray said.

"Ray . . . ," I prompted, trying to remind him of something that happened a couple of seasons ago.

"Okay. I've only ever hit *one* of my customers, and he took the first swing, and he was bigger than I was, and believe me, he really, *really* deserved it."

"How are we supposed to treat Victoria?" I asked.

"I suspect that will not be an issue," Albert said. "You have probably already discovered that she is a very different type of person."

"Very different," I said.

"She is almost always hard-working, conscientious, polite and will do more than expected."

"I'll vouch for that," I said. "We had a really good talk last night."

Albert gave me a questioning look.

"After you two went to sleep," Ray explained. "They must have sat by the fire for more than an hour, just the two of them."

"I was not aware of that," Nigel said.

"You two were sleeping pretty good, judging by the snoring coming from your tent," I said.

"It's nice the kids get along," Ray said.

"Yes . . . nice . . . very nice," Nigel said, although the look on his face and his tone of voice didn't match the words.

"We appreciate that you have befriended the Princess," Albert said. "But it is extremely important that you understand the parameters of the relationship."

"I don't even understand that sentence," I said.

"That makes two of us," Ray agreed.

Albert and Nigel exchanged a look.

"Let me try to explain this," Albert said. "You must be aware that your interaction with any member of the Royal Family is governed by very specific protocols and—"

"You're losing me again," Ray said. "Do you understand what he means?"

"No idea," I agreed.

Albert looked as though he was struggling to come up with the right words. "There are constraints . . . limitations . . . restrictions . . . actions that are prohibited."

"Oh, I understand," Ray said.

"Excellent!"

"You don't want us to clock her, either."

"Of course I don't, but that is not what I am referring to in this instance!" Albert was beginning to sound frustrated.

"Then maybe you'd better just spit it out in good plain Canadian English," Ray snapped.

Once again Albert and Nigel exchanged a long look.

"Let me handle it," Nigel said. He turned to me. "You cannot kiss the Princess."

"Why can't he?" Ray demanded.

"I haven't . . . I won't . . . I don't want to!" I sputtered.

"Why don't you?" Ray asked. "She's a pretty little thing, and you two are the same age and all."

"Regardless," Albert said, "it would not be appropriate."

"I won't! Honestly!"

"Thank you so much. We appreciate your cooperation in this most delicate matter," Nigel said.

"Can I ask a question?" Ray said.

"Certainly," Albert replied.

"If she kisses him, is he allowed to kiss her back?"

"She would not do that," Albert said.

"Why wouldn't she? Don't you think my cousin is good enough for her?"

"No, I was not implying that!"

"So you *do* think he's good enough for her then?"

Albert looked flustered and confused. He took a deep breath. "It is not a question of who is good enough or not good enough, it is simply a fact of life that she is a princess and must be treated as such. Understood?"

"That's no problem for me," I assured him.

"And for you?" Albert asked Ray.

Ray shrugged. "I'm not planning on kissing *any* of you. Now, if you don't mind, how about if we get them up and get on with our day."

I followed Ray's lead and started to angle in toward the shore. Although it was hidden from view around a slight outcrop of land, I knew there was a river just ahead. It was a short stretch connecting this lake to the next.

"Are we heading to shore?" Victoria asked.

"Have to. We're running out of lake. We'll portage around some rapids."

"Are they big rapids?" she asked.

"Not too bad. I've been down them before."

"Do you think you could navigate those rapids with me here in the bow?" she asked.

"Probably."

"Then why don't we try?"

Up ahead, Ray and Andrew had disappeared around the little point of land.

"Lots of reasons."

"Like what?" she asked.

"For one, you're still not very experienced."

"But you've been telling me how well I've been doing all morning!" she protested.

"And you are. Second reason, Ray didn't say we could."

"And if I could convince him?" she asked.

"That would still leave us the third reason."

"And what is that?"

We rounded the point and the river opened up right in front of us.

"And the third reason is that the river flows *into* this lake and I've never met anybody who could paddle up a rapids."

She turned around and scowled at me and I started to laugh. She took her paddle and splashed water up at me, spraying my face.

"Hey!" I yelled.

She splashed me again.

"Cut it out!"

"And if I don't?"

"Well . . . Hey, stop it!" I yelled as she hit me with another blast of water.

"What are you going to do about it?" she asked again.

"I'm going to do this!"

I put all my weight on one side of the canoe, practically pushing it down to the waterline and then quickly shifted to the other side, almost causing the canoe to tip. Victoria screamed.

"You going to stop? Or are we going in?" I yelled.

"Never!" she hollered, and she splashed me.

I cupped my hand and tossed up a handful of water that hit her in the back of the head. She turned away and I splashed her again, and again, and again!

"I surrender!" she screamed.

I splashed her once more for good measure.

"You win! I quit . . . honestly!"

"The person in the back of the canoe is always going to win," I pointed out.

"I believe you. Maybe *I* should paddle in the back tomorrow."

"You need a little more experience before that can— do you hear something?"

She perked up her ears and looked around. "Just the sound of the river. Wait, I do hear something. It sounds like a motorboat."

"Not a motorboat. A plane." I scanned the sky but I couldn't see anything.

"Do you think it could be your father?" Victoria asked.

"There's a good chance. There aren't that many pilots who fly into here."

"Over there!" Victoria said, pointing.

Coming up behind us, still far off over the lake, was a plane. It was too far away to see much about it, but it certainly wasn't orange, so it wasn't my father. It was coming in fast and low, almost straight toward us.

"I don't recognize the plane," I said, over the increasing noise of the engine.

What I could tell was that it was a large float plane. It looked as though it could probably hold eight or ten people. As it passed overhead I could see there were two canoes secured on the top of the floats. Victoria waved up at it.

I wasn't sure who these people were, or where they had come from, but I was willing to bet the plane was going into the bush to drop off some fishermen who didn't want to have to paddle in.

"That was a big plane."

"Bigger than my father's. A plane that size could have come from as far away as Calgary . . . maybe even farther."

In the distance the plane began to bank. I watched as it started a long, slow circle back. It seemed to be circling right around us.

"He's checking us out," I said.

"Why would he be doing that?" Victoria asked.

"Probably making sure we're okay. When you waved he might have thought you were trying to get his attention."

"I was just trying to be friendly."

The plane completed a full circle and then broke off and headed in the direction it had been going before it saw us. It got smaller and smaller, and the noise from the engines became just a gentle buzz and then faded to nothing. Finally I lost sight of it.

"That's certainly a faster way to move," I said.

"I greatly prefer our method of travel."

"Is that so?"

"Yes, I do," she said firmly.

"In that case, how about you put that paddle in the water and we start travelling again."

"Yes, sir!" she said, and saluted me. "Right away, sir!"

"That's more like the kind of treatment I deserve. It's about time you showed me a little respect."

Something told me it was no accident when her next paddle stroke skimmed the surface and soaked me, but good!

CHAPTER EIGHT

THE PORTAGE AROUND THE RAPIDS WAS SHORT and sweet. Ray made darn sure that Andrew took his share of the load, and Albert and Nigel demonstrated that they didn't just look strong. I couldn't believe how much they could carry.

We put the canoes back in the water and paddled less than a kilometre before we put in to make camp for the night. It was a beautiful spot, slightly up on a hill where a breeze kept the bugs away, with a supply of wood close by, a little stream flowing in and a very gentle beach, where we could wash up and even take a swim. Finally, when the camp was set up and supper was ready, we sat down to eat.

"How many kilometres did we do today?" Victoria asked.

"Close to thirty," Ray said. "We could have done more if I wasn't carrying so much dead weight," he added looking pointedly at Andrew.

"I tried hard today . . . much harder than yesterday," Andrew protested.

"Unless you were dead you'd have to work harder than yesterday," Ray said.

Andrew looked hurt.

"But you are learning," Ray conceded. "By the end of this trip you might be halfway good."

Andrew perked up. "You really think I could be good?"

"I said halfway good. The other half I'm not so sure about. But who knows, with enough practice you might make it all the way."

"Speaking of practice," Victoria said, "could I have a turn paddling in the back of the canoe tomorrow?"

"Not without more instruction," Ray said. "When you paddle stern, you're responsible for steering the canoe. But there's still more than an hour of light left. Do you think you could handle some more time on the water?"

"Sure!" she said.

Ray stood up. "Good. Jamie, take her out on the lake for a short paddle and give her some instruction."

"Perhaps I can go as well," Albert said, rising to his feet. I knew he didn't want me to be alone with Victoria.

"Why?" Ray asked. "You're doing okay, but you're not good enough to be teaching anybody." He turned to Andrew. "You want to get better than halfway good?"

"Sure."

"Then you go too. Vicky can be in the stern, you'll be up in the bow, and Jamie will be in the middle, where he can tell you both what you're doing wrong. Is that okay with you, Al?"

"Well . . ."

"It's not like they're going anywhere. Jamie will just take them out a bit and then bring them on back. It's a good way to develop a little character, don't you think?"

*   *   *

"Try to make your strokes longer," I said to Andrew.

"If you don't like the way I'm doing it, maybe you should take the paddle," he offered.

"Not me. I'm just a passenger—and it might be a little bit easier if you put down that can of bug spray."

"No way."

"How about my paddling?" Victoria asked.

"I'm sure my precious sister is doing just wonderfully," Andrew chipped in.

"Actually, her J-stroke should be more the way I showed you. If you did it right you wouldn't have to switch from side to side to keep us going in a straight line."

"I have to switch because my brother combines a lack of effort with a lack of skill," she snapped. "I'm having to canoe for three people."

"Shut up!"

"No, you shut up!" she said.

"Both of you shut up! If you want to fight, go back to camp! If you want to learn to canoe better, then stay here and stay quiet!"

They both closed their mouths.

We started to move a little better and rounded a point, putting us out of sight of the camp. I was having them keep us fairly close to the shore, following the ins and outs of the land to improve their paddling technique. I could just picture Albert and Nigel standing on the shore, peering into the distance, panicking because they'd lost sight of us.

Of course I didn't know what they were more afraid

of—something terrible happening, or me kissing Victoria. What a joke that was! I'd never kissed anybody except my mother or grandmother. It wasn't like I was some sort of dangerous serial smoocher. There was one girl at school—Fiona was her name—who wanted me to kiss her . . . at least I was pretty sure she wanted me to. She didn't actually ask me to kiss her or anything, but I could tell . . . I guess.

I thought maybe I wanted to as well, but I just wasn't sure how to go about it. It looked so clumsy, and I couldn't figure out for sure where the two noses went. Was there some sort of kissing rule, or did you just hope that one person's nose went one way and the other person's the other? Maybe it was like a pop fly in baseball and somebody called it. It would be awful if you bumped and one or both of you got a bleeding nose. That wouldn't be a very magical moment.

"Is this better?" Victoria asked.

I turned around. I couldn't help looking straight at her lips. She looked very pretty.

"Well?"

"Well, what?"

"My paddling? Am I doing better?"

I turned back around, away from her. Had she noticed I was staring at her . . . at her lips? Maybe the secret was to just keep looking forward at the back of Andrew's head.

She tapped me on the shoulder. "So, Jamie, are you going to give me your expert opinion?"

Reluctantly I turned toward her and I found myself once again looking at her lips. In desperation I looked down and instantly realized that I shouldn't be staring at that part of her body either.

"You're doing great," I said, and spun back around.

"You didn't even see me paddle!"

"I have to watch Andrew for a while," I sputtered. "He needs my help more."

They continued to paddle away and I continued to try to focus on not thinking about Victoria sitting behind me. We weren't more than a foot apart. I could hear her breathing. Maybe if I took a really, really deep breath I could even smell her, I thought. She had some kind of bug spray on—I think it was Deep Woods Off. Somehow, though, on her, it smelled good. I wondered if she ever wore perfume . . . of course she wore perfume, she was a princess! She probably had a whole room full of stuff like that. For sure she at least used some type of scented deodorant—darn, why hadn't I packed some deodorant on this trip? I must have smelled awful. Maybe tomorrow I could get up early and wash up.

"Jamie, which way should we go?" Victoria asked.

"Just follow the shore."

"Shouldn't we go out more? We're awfully close to—"

"Just who's in charge here anyway?" I asked.

"Fine," she said. "We'll stay in by the shore."

If I only had deodorant, it wouldn't be so bad sitting in the canoe. And maybe some more clean clothes. And a comb. And some breath mints would have been fantastic. It would be better to kiss somebody if you had a TicTac in your mouth—what was I thinking! I wasn't going to kiss her. I wasn't going to try to kiss her. I wasn't even going to *think* about kissing her. Okay, I was going to think about it, but I didn't really have much choice. It was like somebody saying "Don't think of elephants," and then elephants are the only thing you can think of.

I didn't even know if she wanted me to kiss her. Maybe she was just being friendly. Princesses are trained to be friendly. Being around my grandmother, I'd been forced to look at enough pictures and videos to know that they all seemed to have that same smile pasted on their faces all the time. Maybe she didn't like me, maybe she was simply acting the way a princess was supposed to act toward one of her subjects. I remembered that she'd said she always had to act polite. On the other hand, one of the guys at school told me that one of the girls at school told him that some of the girls—she wouldn't say who—think I'm pretty good-looking because I'm tall for my age and my hair looks good when I let it grow long and I've got a nice smile . . . well, she *did* say that, not me—

"Jamie, what do we do now?" Victoria exclaimed.

I snapped out of my thoughts. "We just—jeez, the river!" We were right at the river. The walls of the banks rose up high on both sides.

"I can't get us out of the current, and—"

"Paddle harder!" I yelled. "Andrew, paddle on the other side. Victoria, try to steer us across the current so we don't get sucked in!"

The canoe swung into the little mouth of the river and I felt my stomach rise up into my throat as we dropped down the first little bump.

"Jamie, do something!" Andrew screamed.

"Can't you turn it around or bring us to shore?" Victoria asked.

"Look around; there's no place. The shore is too high already."

"Surely there must be someplace where—"

"We're going through the rapids," I said.

"Oh my dear God." Victoria's voice was just barely audible over the increasing roar of the water.

We were on a little stretch of flat water, but the river was getting faster as it was squeezing through the narrows.

"Both of you put on your life jackets! Quickly! There's not much time."

They pulled them off the floor and started to put them on. I only wished I'd put three life jackets in the canoe.

"My paddle! I dropped my paddle!" Andrew screamed.

I thrust my hand into the water to try to grab it as it floated past us, but it was too far away.

"Here, take mine!" Victoria shouted.

"It won't do him any good!" I yelled.

"No, *you* take the paddle! *You* steer!"

"I can't steer from the middle!"

"But—*aaaahhhh!*" Victoria screamed as we dropped over a big dip.

My stomach flipped again. I couldn't panic. I had to think about what was up ahead. I'd been through these rapids before, once before, years ago. I realized I had no idea what was coming.

We hit another dip and the canoe bucked, the water rose up, and we seemed to be turning to the side.

"Straighten us out!" I screamed. "Keep us going straight!"

"I don't know how!" she hollered.

Suddenly we slammed into a rock and I felt myself being thrown forward. I grabbed onto the side of the canoe to stop myself from getting airborne and it dipped down. Water came pouring in over the side. The canoe whirled around the rock and I looked forward— or backwards. We were heading through the rapids turned backwards!

I spun in my seat so I was facing the right way, down the rapids and toward Victoria. She was soaking wet, with her hair plastered down and a look of total panic on her face.

"Give me the paddle!" I hollered. "Give it to me!"

She practically tossed it at me like it was on fire.

The canoe bucked and rocked over another dip. I'd anchored my feet under the seat, but Victoria bounced up into the air, and for a second I was positive she was going to go over the side.

"Turn around in your seat!" I yelled. "And then hold on with your feet as well as your hands!"

She had just started to turn when the canoe seemed to drop right away, and she was in mid-air above the seat. I lunged forward and grabbed her by the waist and pulled her back down. Then there was a shudder and the sound of grinding, and the whole canoe bounced off to the side.

I let go of Victoria and grabbed the paddle again. Desperately I scanned forward and . . . and . . . there was only lake.

"We made it," Victoria said. "We made it!"

"We did?" Andrew asked from behind me.

I turned partway around. Andrew was sitting there, still looking backwards, frozen in place. The whole bottom half of the canoe was filled with water. I knew we'd taken on water, but—

"We ran the rapids, and we're no worse for wear," Victoria said.

"Maybe *you* survived," I muttered.

"What do you mean?"

"Look at the canoe. There's a hole."

"Where?" Victoria asked.

I pointed. There was a gash on the side—a big gash— just behind where she sat. Water was pouring in.

"Can it be repaired?"

"I don't know. We have to get to shore before we sink completely."

"Sink? We're going to sink!" Andrew exclaimed.

"Shut up, Andrew!" I yelled. I dug the paddle in and propelled us toward the shore. I dug in again, and again, and again. The canoe was so heavy with water—and filling up by the second—that there was no way I was getting us to shore.

"There's too much weight," I said. "Andrew, get out of the canoe."

"You want me to get into the water?" he asked in amazement.

"You have a life jacket on. Just swim to shore."

"But why me? Why doesn't my sister have to go?"

"You're right. She should go."

"I should?" Victoria asked.

"You *both* have to go. Get out of the canoe. Now!"

Victoria didn't say another word. She just zipped her life jacket up to the top and slipped over the edge of the canoe and into the water.

"You too, Andrew," I said.

He grumbled and groaned.

"Look, Andrew, either you get out and I have a chance to get the canoe to shore, or you stay put and it sinks. Either way, you're going to be swimming."

"Get out, Andrew!" Victoria screamed. "Come on and we'll swim in together. You'll be just fine. It isn't far."

Reluctantly he slipped over the side. In one hand, he was still clutching his can of bug spray.

With both of them gone, the canoe rose up slightly out of the water. Unfortunately, the gash was still below the waterline, and it would be only a matter of time before it filled up completely and sank.

I dug the paddle in once more. Even with the two of them gone, the weight of the water was still tremendous, and the canoe was barely budging with each stroke. Up ahead Victoria and Andrew were almost all

the way to shore, wading through the shallows. They
weren't that far away, and if I could just get the canoe
that far, even if it sank, I could still drag it to the shore
and it wouldn't be lost.

I dug in deep and strained with all my might, but the
canoe barely moved. Maybe if I jumped out I could
swim and tow it along behind me. I grabbed the rope
and rolled over the side. The canoe bobbed up slightly,
but the craft was still taking on water. I struggled
forward. It felt like I was dragging an anchor . . . I *was*
dragging an anchor. The canoe was sinking fast, and
now it was barely peeking out of the water behind me.
This wasn't going to work. I stopped swimming and
tried to touch the bottom. I couldn't do it. I had to get
farther in. I started to swim and—

"Let me help you!" Victoria was calling from the
water just a few metres away.

"You're supposed to be on shore."

"I got Andrew in safely and I came back out to help
you."

"I don't need any help."

"Sure you don't," she snapped.

She swam up. Then she reached down and grabbed
hold of the rope, just above where I was holding it.
"Now let's get going."

Together we tugged at the canoe. It seemed to be
moving better. Not well, but better than it had.

"How much farther until it gets shallow?" I asked,
panting with each word.

"Too far. Maybe we should just leave the canoe."

"Can't . . . not my canoe."

"Ray will understand."

"Ha!" I snapped, despite my tiredness.

"Wouldn't he rather you survived than one of his canoes?" she asked.

"Hard to say."

"But it's smashed anyway."

"Can be fixed . . . I think . . . but if it sinks in deep water it's gone."

"What if we mark where it sinks?" she asked.

"How?"

Without answering Victoria stopped swimming and started to tread water. She sank lower into the water.

"What are you doing?'

"This," she said as she handed me her life jacket. "Tie this to the rope and it will mark the spot where the canoe goes down."

"It'll only mark it if the rope is longer than the water is deep."

"How long is the rope?" Victoria asked.

"About four metres."

"The water doesn't look that deep."

"It's hard to judge really clean water. It could be a lot deeper."

"Either way, tie it on, because by all indications the canoe is going to sink."

I looked back. There was no question that she was right. The only direction this canoe was going was down. Quickly I looped the rope through the buckle of the jacket. I pulled it taut and then struggled to keep my head above water while I used both hands to tie a double knot and pull it tight.

"Come on, let's get to shore," Victoria said.

"Can't . . . have to wait until it sinks . . . see if the jacket marks it."

"That sounds utterly pointless," she said. "Either it will work or it will not, and there is nothing you can do. Now come, before *you* sink!"

I wanted to argue, but I knew she was right. My arms were suddenly feeling heavy and I didn't know how long I could stay out there and still reach the shore. I flipped over on my back and let my arms dangle beside me, kicking my legs to propel me forward. As I moved I looked up at the sky. It was still light, and the sun was circling the horizon, but the moon was already in the sky. What was I going to say to Ray? What was Ray going to say to me?

"You can put your feet down now," Victoria said.

I spun around and stood up. My feet sank into the muddy bottom. I struggled forward and tripped. Victoria grabbed my arm and steadied me. I expected her to let go, but she continued to hold on as the water got shallower and shallower. I waded out and collapsed on the shore, beside Andrew. Victoria came and sat down beside me.

"The important thing is that we have all survived," Victoria said.

"So far," I said.

"What do you mean?" Andrew asked apprehensively.

"I don't know who I should be more afraid of," I said,

"Ray, when he finds out that I wrecked one of his canoes, or Albert and Nigel, when they hear that I almost drowned you two."

"Don't worry about the canoe," Victoria said. "We will make sure that full restitution is made."

"What?"

"We will pay for a replacement canoe if this one can't be fixed," she said. "And as for our two body-guards, they will not be angry at you. They will be most grateful that your heroic actions saved our lives."

"Saved your lives?" I asked in disbelief.

"But of course. If not for you we both could very well have perished in the rapids," she said.

"If it hadn't been for me, you would never have been in the rapids to begin with. That was my fault. I'm responsible."

"We were all in the canoe."

"But it was my responsibility to keep you two safe. I should never have let you get so close to the mouth of the rapids . . . I wasn't paying attention."

"You did seem rather distracted, but it was not your fault."

"Then whose fault was it?"

"Mine."

"Yours?"

She nodded her head. "I knew you weren't paying attention. I knew we were getting close to the rapids. I knew we shouldn't be there . . . but . . ."

"You wanted to shoot the rapids, didn't you?"

Again she nodded. "I thought we could do it."

"Why would you think that?" I demanded as I rose to my feet.

"It didn't look that difficult as we portaged around it, and you said that you had been through it before, and—"

"Yes, I'd been through it before, with Ray! That doesn't mean that you and your brother could do it!"

"But you were in the canoe too."

"In the middle, without a paddle! How could you even think that—?"

"I am sorry."

"You're sorry?" I demanded.

"Truly, truly, sorry," she said, and smiled at me.

"I . . . I . . . I . . . forget it . . . just forget it. Come on, we have to get back before it gets dark."

CHAPTER NINE

"I DIDN'T THINK that we'd paddled this far," Victoria said.

"We didn't," I answered. "The route by water was a lot shorter. More direct."

"But we are going in the correct direction, aren't we?" Andrew asked. He sounded anxious.

"We're fine."

"As will be the canoe," Victoria said.

I didn't know that for sure, but I did know that the life jacket that I'd tied on was bobbing at the surface, marking the spot where it went down. As we were walking I kept rehearsing what I was going to say to Ray, how I was going to explain to him what happened. I guess I should have been more worried about what Albert and Nigel were going to say—or do. I was pretty sure they weren't going to shoot me, but part of me still wondered. In the old days, didn't they cut off the heads of people who caused problems for the Royal Family?

I could picture Albert and Nigel going totally ballistic when we didn't return. We should have been back almost two hours ago. They were probably out in the canoes looking for us right now, yelling out our names. But I hadn't heard anything. And sound really travels up

in the bush, and we weren't that far away . . . or were
we? I stopped. We *were* going in the right direction . . .
I was pretty sure.

"What's wrong?" Andrew asked.

"What makes you think anything's wrong?"

"You stopped. Why did you stop?"

"I just wanted to get my bearings," I said.

"Bearings, as in we're lost?"

"We're not lost," I said.

"Then why did you stop?"

"You looked like you needed a rest," I lied.

"He *always* looks like he needs a rest," Victoria said.

"Shut up!" he snapped.

"Both of you shut up! I need some quiet to think."

"Think about what?" Andrew demanded anxiously.

"Think about why I didn't just let you drown so I could
get some peace," I said. "I just want to make sure that
we're going the shortest and easiest route back to the
camp, and I have to think to do that. Unless you want to
go a longer and harder way, or you think you should lead?"

"Me? No way!"

"Good. Just sit there and be quiet then. It's better
you're quiet anyway. The big grizzlies like to feed about
now." Of course that was a lie. The big grizzlies feed all
the time.

I tried to picture exactly where we were in relation to
the campsite. There was no question we were going in the
right direction. The safest route would have been to
simply travel along the shore, but that was also the longest
route. I'd tried to save us distance, and now I wondered if

I'd steered us too far into the forest. Maybe we'd bypassed the camp already. If we were even close to the lake we should have heard them calling for us. I could correct that by just taking us straight to the left. We couldn't help but hit the lake if we did that. Unfortunately the sun was starting down. It wasn't going to set for hours still—not till about two in the morning—but it was much dimmer when it skimmed the horizon. Besides, the longer I was away, the more worried everybody would be, and the more trouble I'd be in when we finally got there.

"I think we should just continue with your original plan," Victoria said.

"What?"

"I am positive you are taking us on the correct course. Don't let doubts confuse you or cloud your judgment."

I was going to say something, deny that I was even having second thoughts, but I knew that she knew. The strangest thing was that I was the one experienced in the bush, the one who lived up here, the one who was Native, and I should have been the one trying to reassure her. Instead, she was doing the reassuring. She seemed so calm about the whole thing. I guess I'd just assumed because she was so nervous about the plane ride that she'd be nervous about everything. Of course, she had reason to be nervous about airplanes.

"Perhaps it would be best if we continued on our trek," she said. "I believe we have worried Albert and Nigel enough to last a lifetime."

I started off, and Andrew fell in behind me so close that he bumped into my leg and I stumbled.

"Frightfully sorry," he said.

I was going to say something, but I didn't. Maybe I shouldn't have been telling him all that bear stuff. In all the years I'd lived here, I'd only seen a grizzly a few dozen times myself, and never up close.

"I cannot wait to change into dry apparel," Andrew said.

"What?"

"Clothing," Victoria said. "He wants to get into dry clothes. Perhaps he could start by removing his life jacket. There is very little chance of your drowning while we are on land, Andrew."

Sheepishly he undid the zipper and buckles and removed the jacket.

"Dry clothes would be nice. I'm starting to get a little bit chilly," I said.

"It's amazing how the temperature drops when the sun begins to set," she said.

"Yeah. And after the dry clothes, a big fire to warm ourselves at would be even better," I added.

"And hot cocoa," Andrew suggested.

"I don't know about cocoa, but I'd love a cup of hot coffee right now. Of course, I don't know whether I'd drink it or dip my feet in it."

"Is Ray going to be worried?" Victoria asked.

"He'll be worried, but he knows I'll take care of us. I'm more worried about your two bodyguards."

"We'll just point out to them that we are safe and sound and none the worse for the experience," Victoria suggested, sensibly.

"Sounds good," I said. "Now keep repeating it until it sounds believable enough to convince those two not to shoot me."

I kept us moving until we came to a small stream. I knew this stream—at least I thought I did. I was sure it was the one that entered the lake just beside where we'd set up camp. All we had to do was follow it down and we'd be able to see the camp. I was 100 percent sure. Well, almost 100 percent sure. There was no point in saying anything to the others now.

I crossed over the shallow stream, jumping from rock to rock. I guess that it didn't make too much sense to try and stay dry now, since I was practically soaked to the skin, but still . . .

"So," Victoria began, "you think that Ray will be able to fix the canoe."

"Probably."

"And will he have the materials with him to do that?" she asked.

"He always carries some resin and fibreglass strips to fix little gashes," I answered.

"Enough to fix a big gash?"

"Maybe."

"I hope so. I would not like our adventure to be over prematurely," she said.

I shrugged. "Either way, the two remaining canoes are big enough to carry all six of us."

"I see," she said. "And how would you imagine he would divide us up?"

"Can't say for sure, but my guess is that it won't be

me, you and Andrew in the same canoe."

Victoria burst into laughter. "I would suspect you are correct. But maybe you and I will be travelling together?"

"Maybe. With Albert sitting in the middle right between us."

"Yes, he'd like that. He is very protective of me."

"I guess that's what bodyguards do," I admitted.

"It certainly is his vocation, but at times he appears to be overly zealous in his work."

"Yeah," I answered, not really quite sure exactly what she'd just said.

"Look!" Andrew called out. "Over there, I see light . . . a fire!"

Up ahead, off to the side and partially blocked by trees and bushes, I could make out flames. It was a campfire . . . our campfire . . . our campsite! I wanted to yell out in delight, but I needed to stay calm and cool.

"What did you expect?" I asked. "I told you I knew where I was going."

Andrew moved out in front and we doubled our pace, sticking close to the stream. As we closed in two things became obvious: we were still a distance from the camp, and the fire was enormous.

"We'll certainly be able to warm ourselves by that fire," Victoria commented.

"It is gigantic. Ray's probably used up all the wood we gathered," I said. "I guess he wanted it big enough for us to see it in the distance in case we got turned around or something."

"Would they hear us if we yelled from here?" Andrew asked.

"They would, but no yelling. I want us to walk into camp nice and quiet and calm, like nothing much is wrong. Okay?"

"If that's what you wish," Victoria said.

"And let me do the talking, at least to start," I added.

We kept moving toward the fire. The tents became visible and the other two canoes were sitting on the shore, upside down, waiting for us to set off at dawn and . . . why couldn't I see anybody? Where was Ray or Nigel or Albert? Why weren't they standing there at the water's edge, looking for us, calling out? It didn't make sense. They wouldn't have just gone to sleep.

"Hold on," I said as I reached out and grabbed Andrew by the arm. "Just wait."

"I don't want to wait. I want to get into dry clothing and—"

"And keep your voice down."

"Why in God's name would I . . . is it a bear?" he asked, ending his sentence barely above a whisper.

"Just stop and listen to me for a second."

"Is something wrong, Jamie?" Victoria asked.

I crouched down, and they both did the same. "Do either of you see anybody at the campsite? Do you see Ray or Albert or Nigel?"

"No," Victoria said. "I just assumed that they were out trying to locate us."

"Out in what? The canoes are both there," I said.

"Well . . . perhaps they are on foot searching through the forest and—"

"That makes even less sense. There's no way they'd look in the forest when we left by water. Besides, even if they did go out looking, one person would have stayed at the camp."

"Somebody must be close by to keep that fire going so brightly," Victoria said.

"I agree. So where are they?"

"Well, surely there must be a logical explanation," Victoria said.

"If there is I'd really appreciate you sharing it with me."

Nobody said a word.

"I am chilled to the bone," Andrew said, and he started to rise to his feet. "Let's just go and—"

"Nobody's going anywhere," I hissed as I grabbed him and pulled him back down.

"I know that you are fearful of your reception when we arrive, Jamie, but we must go forward," Victoria said.

"I'd be an idiot not to be worried, but that's not what's on my mind now."

"We cannot simply stay here," Victoria said.

"We're not. You two are. I need to get a closer look."

"Jamie, what is it that you expect to see?" she asked.

"I don't know. But it doesn't seem right. Just stay here and stay quiet."

"I don't really understand why . . . but we'll do as you ask."

* * *

I couldn't help thinking that I was acting like an idiot. What did I suspect I'd find at the camp? Was I just letting my imagination get the better of me because I really was scared of what Ray and Albert were going to say? Of course I was scared, but that didn't change the facts. Why weren't they either out looking for us, or standing there by the tents calling out our names?

I moved farther away from the stream bed and into the cover of the woods. I wanted to come at the camp from the back, out of the forest and as far away from the lake as possible. It seemed important not to be seen or heard.

As I moved I felt my heart pounding in my chest and my breath was short. I wasn't moving *that* fast. But this wasn't about how hard I was working, it was about what I was thinking. I was scared, and that fear had nothing to do with what anybody was going to say to me.

I moved slowly, staying low to the ground, going from bush to bush. The sun was still in the sky but it was so low that everything, no matter how small, cast a long shadow. I worked to stay in those shadows. At one point I stopped and slumped down silently to the ground. I tried to control my breathing. I felt myself shaking. This was crazy. Why was I so nervous?

I looked up and caught the silhouette of somebody coming out of the forest and moving toward the fire. Was it Albert? No, it wasn't. I didn't think it was Nigel either, and it definitely wasn't Ray. Who was it? Suddenly, the man turned toward me and I could see he was holding something in his left hand. I'm no expert, but it looked to me like it was a gun, a revolver.

CHAPTER TEN

MY MIND RACED. Had I stumbled into the wrong site and then made a whole lot of wrong conclusions? That would have explained why nobody was there, why I didn't see them looking or calling for us. I felt a rush of relief. Somehow I'd managed to wander into the only other camp within a hundred kilometres of ours. What were the odds of that?

I slowly looked around the site. I was close to the last tent. It certainly looked like one of our tents. Actually, all three of them looked like our tents. They even seemed to be pitched in about the same spots. And the canoes . . . two red canoes up on the shore. My sense of relief was replaced by a chill that ran up my spine. This *was* our camp. But who was that man, and why did he have a gun? Maybe when we went missing, Albert and Nigel sent out word and brought in a search party . . . but they didn't have any way of calling in outside help, did they? And even if they did, how could anybody have got here so fast?

The man tossed a log on the fire and it threw sparks and ashes up into the air. He then turned and headed back into the forest, where he disappeared among the shadows. It almost looked like he was trying to hide.

This was making less and less sense. I had to fight the urge to slip further back into the woods. But then what would we do, sleep in the forest? Besides, my curiosity—my need to figure this out—was greater than any fear I was feeling.

Moving on all fours I began to creep forward again. The long shadows from the trees led all the way to the back of the closest tent. I moved slowly toward it. I didn't know what I hoped to find, but I couldn't think of anything else to do.

I moved without a sound. The only noises were the crackling of the fire, the wind through the trees and the lapping of the water against the shore. I tried to keep one eye on the tent and the other on the place where I'd seen the figure vanish. I didn't see him—of course, that didn't mean I wasn't visible to him. Then again, whoever he was, he wasn't going to be looking for anybody creeping into the campsite from the forest. His eyes would be on the lake, looking for our canoe to return.

I came up behind the tent, grateful that I'd finally reached cover. I slumped down to the ground so that I was as flat as I could possibly get. I suddenly felt exhausted. My breath was short and I felt myself shaking—was it from the damp clothes and the chill or from fear? Silently I took a deep breath, and then another and another. I just needed to steady myself before I went any farther, or— I heard a rustling sound, soft and muffled. I stopped breathing completely and pressed myself even harder into the ground, hoping a hole would just open up and swallow me. The noise came again . . . it sounded like it was coming from the tent. Somebody was *inside* the tent I was hiding behind.

The small back flap was open no more than a metre from my head. I had to look in. I had to. I pushed myself up on my hands, raising my head toward the little screen window and peered inside. It was darker inside than out and I couldn't really see anything. I pressed my face against the mesh. Still nothing . . .

"Jamie?"

I felt a bolt of electricity shoot through me.

"Jamie . . . is that you?" came the whispered voice from inside the tent.

"Ray?" I asked, my voice barely loud enough for me to hear.

"It's Albert."

"Where's Ray?"

"I'm here." This time it was Ray's voice.

"I'm sorry about what happened, and—"

"Be quiet!" Albert snapped. "Just listen. Where are Victoria and Andrew? Are they safe?"

"Yeah, they're in the forest. I'm sorry that—"

"Be still!" he snapped, his voice still a whisper, but threatening.

"Listen to him," Ray said. "Just listen."

I took a deep breath and kept my tongue still.

"Jamie, you have to take Victoria and Andrew and get away."

"Get away? I . . . I don't understand," I sputtered.

"There are men—four men. We are prisoners, tied and bound."

"I saw one of them," I whispered.

"They are all armed. They are here to harm the children, to kidnap or kill them. You can't allow that to happen."

I felt like I'd been hit in the head with a hammer. I understood the words he was saying, but none of them seemed real.

"Do you understand?" Albert asked.

I didn't answer.

"Jamie?"

"Yes?"

"You have to get away."

"Away?" I repeated. "Back home?"

"No," Ray said. "That's what they'd expect. Go the other direction. Head for the fishing lodge up Bass Lake, McGregor's. And stay off the lake. They have a plane. They'll spot you if you go out on the water."

I really didn't have much choice, but this probably wasn't the time to tell him about the canoe.

"You have to go through the forest. Can you do that?"

I didn't answer. That was a long way, and I'd never covered it on the ground.

"Can you do that, Jamie?" Albert asked.

"I can try," I said, hoping I sounded more confident than I felt. "But what about you and Ray and Nigel?"

"It's just me and Albert," Ray said.

"Nigel got away?" I asked. Maybe I could catch up with him and he could help me take care of everything.

"Nigel is dead," Albert said. "He was shot, and—"

Albert stopped as we both heard the same sound—footsteps coming toward the tent. I heard the zipper open, a faint light came in, and I ducked down away from the window.

"Where are they?" a voice demanded. It wasn't loud, but there was a forceful, scary feeling to it. He had an accent. Was it an English accent?

"I shall tell you nothing more than the nothing I have told you thus far," Albert said. He sounded calm, in control.

"Your loyalty is admirable," the man said. "But ultimately you will tell us the information we require or pay the consequences for your—"

"Hey, buddy," Ray said, cutting him off. "I ain't got no reason to protect those kids. It isn't like the Royal Family has done anything for us Natives except steal our land."

The man laughed. "As they have stolen from many peoples around the world."

"Do not tell him anything!" Albert said. "Nothing, or—auugggghhh!"

"You will be quiet," the man snapped, "or you'll get it again."

"Like I said, buddy," Ray said, "I don't care about those kids. My friend, the other guide, will be bringing them back soon, tomorrow at the latest. All you have to do is sit right here and they'll come back."

Ray wasn't making a deal with them, he was just trying to get them to stay put so we'd have a chance to get farther away.

"And when my guide brings them back you can take those kids and go. You can just leave us here. It isn't like we can get help. You smash our canoes and it'll take us two weeks to get anyplace where we can tell anybody what happened. Sound like a deal, buddy?"

"I am not sure what you have to offer by way of a deal," the man said.

"I just thought I could help you find them," Ray said. "And then you'll let me and my guide go."

"Not a particularly noble sentiment." The man chuckled. "Regardless, we will locate them."

"Don't be so sure of that," Albert said.

"I am sure," the man replied. "Technology is a wonderful thing."

Technology? What did that mean?

"Now both of you . . . silence."

I heard the sound of the zipper being done up again, and then footsteps moving away. Finally silence. I pushed myself back up so I could peer in through the mesh again.

"Albert? Ray?"

"Jamie," Albert said softly. "Go . . . get away."

"But what about you two?"

"Forget about us," Albert whispered.

"No, don't forget about us," Ray insisted. "Get help and get it fast. That's the only chance we have."

"Now go," Albert said. "You are the only hope any of us has. It is up to you."

CHAPTER ELEVEN

I CRAWLED AWAY FROM THE TENT, leaving Ray and Albert behind. I really wanted to stand up and run for all I was worth, but I couldn't. I had to move slowly, silently. If they saw me, there was no way I could outrun a bullet. Was that what had happened to Nigel?

I made the bushes and felt a sense of relief. I got to my feet but stayed hunched over. I'd have preferred to stay on all fours, but I couldn't very well crawl back to where the others were waiting. I quickly put a layer of trees between the camp and me. Then another layer of trees, and another. With each step I was making myself safer and safer . . . safer from four men with guns . . . four men who were trying to kidnap or kill Victoria and Andrew . . . four men who had killed Nigel . . . killed him. How could that be possible?

I reached the stream and started to splash through the shallow water. I instantly regretted the noise I was making but I was far enough away that I figured I couldn't be heard from the campsite. Besides, at that point, whether I was heard or not there was no way that anybody was going to figure out the direction of the sound and catch me before I got away. I rounded a bend in the stream. More distance. More safety. I just had to find Victoria and Andrew and then—and then what?

"Jamie!"

I practically jumped up into the air as I spun around. Victoria and Andrew had been sitting in some bushes off to the side of the stream and I'd gone right past them.

"So, can we go to the camp now and—?"

"We have to leave," I said. I grabbed Victoria by the hand and started to pull her upstream, away from the camp.

"Wait! What are you doing?" she demanded.

"Keep your voice down!" I pleaded. "We have to get farther away. We have to hide in the forest!"

"We can't do that!" Andrew exclaimed. "I need to get into dry clothes and—"

"We can't go back to the camp!"

"I am sure that Ray and Albert and Nigel are mad, but—"

"Nigel isn't mad," I said. "He's dead."

There was a pause. I could almost hear the two of them thinking about what I'd just said, not able to believe their ears.

"He's dead," I repeated.

"But . . . but how?" Victoria sounded really shaken.

I shook my head. "I don't know. Albert told me."

"You spoke to Albert?"

"I sneaked up to the tent. He and Ray have been taken prisoner. They're in the tent all tied up."

"Then we have to free them," Victoria said.

"There are four guys holding them, and they must have guns. How else could they have overpowered them? There's nothing I can do. Nothing. They told me the only way to get help is to get away and let the authorities know what's happened."

"But surely—"

"There's nothing." I paused, not wanting to say the rest, but knowing I had to. "Albert said that the men . . . he said that the men are here to . . . to . . ."

"To harm Andrew and me," Victoria said.

I nodded my head.

"Albert said it was up to me to protect you and your brother, to lead you to safety."

"Lead us to safety?" Andrew asked. "Where are you going to take us?"

"There's a fishing lodge."

"And we'll be safe there?"

"There'll be people and a radio. They can call the RCMP, call my father to come in and get us out."

"How far is it?" Victoria asked.

"About forty kilometres from here."

"Forty kilometres by water or on foot?"

"We'll have to travel a little farther than that, but not too much farther."

"There must be an alternative," Andrew said.

I shook my head.

"There has to be," he whined. "There *has* to be!"

"There is," I said. "I'll walk to the fishing lodge. Your sister can come with me."

"And what about me?"

"You can either stay right here and wait, or you can go down the stream to the camp and give yourself up. I'm sure they'll give you dry clothes . . . before they do whatever else it is that they're planning to do to you." I paused. "So, what's your choice?"

Andrew didn't answer. He seemed to be speechless—something I really hadn't seen before.

"Let's go," I said. I started upstream, away from the camp.

I turned around and Victoria was right behind me. She was with Andrew, leading him by the hand.

Victoria and Andrew were starting to fall behind. I stopped walking and waited for them. We'd travelled for close to an hour and we'd put a safe distance between us and the guns.

"How are you doing?" I asked as they caught up.

"I am exhausted," Andrew sighed.

"And you?" I asked Victoria.

"Tired."

"We're going to stop now," I said.

"We can keep going if we have to," she said.

I shook my head. "We shouldn't. It's getting too dark."

"It has become difficult to see," she agreed.

"And it's going to go from difficult to impossible soon. We'll stop for a few hours and start again when the sun rises."

"Are we stopping right here?" Andrew asked.

"It's as good a place as any."

"But are we safe?"

"They're not going to find us."

"What about bears?"

"They won't bother us either."

"Shouldn't we have a fire . . . just in case? Bears won't come up to the fire, right?" he asked.

"A fire would be nice," I agreed. "As the sun drops the rest of the way the temperature is going to drop as well. But a fire's not going to happen."

"Why not?" Andrew demanded. "Why can't we have a fire?"

"Do you have any matches on you?" I asked.

"Of course not!"

"A lighter?"

"No!"

"Neither do I," I said. I'd left all my things back at the camp. "Victoria, how about you?"

"Of course not," she answered.

"Then, no matches, no lighter, no fire. Understand?"

"But we *need* a fire," Andrew said.

"I can't just snap my fingers and make a fire appear," I answered.

"But perhaps there is a way that we can have a fire," Victoria said.

"Didn't you just say you didn't have matches?"

"I don't, but I am familiar with some techniques for starting a fire without matches."

I shot her a skeptical look.

"I read about it in a book," she said reluctantly.

"You read about it in a book?"

"It was about survival in the bush."

"Great. And what exactly did it suggest, that you bang two rocks together?"

"Not exactly. What I require is some kindling, like pine needles or really dry grass, and a stick and a shoelace."

"I'm *sure* that will work," I said sarcastically.

She ignored my comment. "I can use the lace off one of my shoes. And I think this stick looks about the same size as the one in the illustration in the book," she said, picking up a stick from the ground.

"And how do that stick and a shoelace produce fire?" I asked.

"Rather than explain, why don't I provide a demonstration. Could you and Andrew gather some materials that I can use as kindling?"

"The only thing I'm gathering is berries," I said.

"Berries?"

"From that patch we just passed. I'm hungry."

"So am I," Andrew agreed. "But I would much rather have something else to eat."

"Then why don't you just ring up the butler or cook or whoever and place a special order? It's berries or nothing. You coming?"

He nodded.

"And you?" I asked Victoria.

"If you don't mind, I think I would prefer to attempt to start a fire."

"You can attempt anything you want, but I think you're wasting your time. You should be thinking about putting something in your stomach and then putting your head down on the ground. The sun will rise in about three and a half hours. As soon as it's up we have to get going."

"I just want to try," she said.

"Knock yourself out. I'll be down in the berry patch. You coming, Andrew?"

He hesitated. "I was just wondering . . . isn't that where the bears are likely to congregate?"

"You mean, like, hang around?"

"Precisely."

"There were none there two minutes ago when we passed through. I doubt there are any there now. But stay here if you want. It's up to you."

I turned and started down the way we'd just come. I didn't hear any steps coming behind me, so I stopped and looked back. Victoria was sitting on the ground. She'd taken off a shoe and was removing the lace. Andrew stood over her, watching.

Fine, I thought, let them try to make a fire. More berries for me.

CHAPTER TWELVE

"UNBELIEVABLE," I MUTTERED.

I could just make out Victoria's outline as I stumbled along the dark forest floor—she was a silhouette against the light thrown from a small fire.

"How did you do that?" I asked as I reached her side. Andrew was lying beside her. He appeared to be asleep.

"The book was right! I used the shoelace to spin the stick, and the stick rubbing against the rock created heat, the heat ignited the needles and *voilà,* I had a fire! Impressed?"

"Impressed . . . but not surprised."

"You *thought* I could make a fire?" she asked.

"Not really, to be honest, but somehow when I saw it I thought, if anybody could have done it, it was you."

She beamed at me. "Thank you. Now come and sit down and warm yourself," she said as she patted the rock beside her.

I stepped over the sleeping Andrew and sat down. The fire wasn't big, but it threw off a beautiful warmth. I felt it start to seep into my toes and work its way up my legs. There was very little smoke, and whatever there was certainly wouldn't be visible to anybody looking for us.

"Perhaps I should have come with you to gather berries. I am frightfully hungry," she said.

I stood up, reached into my pocket and pulled out a partially squashed handful of berries. "Here."

"Thank you," she said as she took them. "I imagine I should save half for Andrew."

"Don't bother," I said. "I have a second pocketful just for him. And we can get some more in the morning."

"I can't believe how good these taste," she said as she put some of the berries in her mouth. "This might be the best thing I have *ever* eaten!"

"That's because you're so hungry."

"And tired," she said as she ate more of the berries.

"Go to sleep. You can at least get a few hours of shut-eye before the sun comes up."

"Are you going to stay up?"

"Me? I'm going to try to sleep too."

"But shouldn't somebody stay awake? Stand guard?"

"I need sleep," I said.

She nodded her head. "Of course you need sleep. We need you to be alert to lead us to safety. I shall stay awake."

"Nobody needs to stay awake."

"But somebody has to be on guard."

"We don't need a guard. Those guys aren't going to find us. They probably aren't even looking yet, because they expect us to return to camp tomorrow. And there's no way any wild animal is going to come this close to a fire. What we need is to sleep. Go to sleep."

I slipped off the rock and snuggled myself into the ground, reaching under my back to remove a stone. It certainly wasn't as comfortable as my bed—or even my sleeping bag—but it still felt good. I closed my eyes.

The side of me closest to the fire felt warm, while the other side, facing away, was chilled. I wished I had a blanket to pull up or a pillow under my head. It would have been nice to have been in my tent . . . my tent. Ray and Albert were in my tent, tied up. They would have given anything to have been here with me. My mind started racing, thinking about everything that had happened. Had it only been a few hours ago that we went through the rapids? A few hours since I saw Ray and Albert all tied up in the tent? A few hours since I found out that Nigel was dead? I sat up.

Victoria was still sitting on the rock. She looked over and smiled.

"It looks like only one of us is able to sleep," she said, gesturing down at her brother, still dozing at her feet.

"At least when he's sleeping he's not talking," I remarked.

"I actually like him best when he is only semiconscious like this. Besides, if I were asleep I would be missing the show."

"The show?"

"Yes, the northern lights. They are magnificent!"

I looked up at the flickers of green light playing in the sky.

"I didn't really notice," I admitted. "I guess I see them so often I just don't pay attention."

"How often are the lights visible?" she asked.

"About two hundred and fifty nights every year."

"They were not visible last night, or the night before," she observed.

"It's rare for them to not be out for three nights in a row. They're the reason a lot of tourists come up here," I said. "Of course, this really isn't much of a show tonight."

"It gets better than this?" she asked in disbelief.

"Lots. Brighter, bigger, and of course different colours. I think it's best when there are yellows and pinks and reds mixed in with the greens."

"That would be amazing! I'd love to see that!"

"Maybe you'll see them tomorrow night. It depends on the conditions."

"Sounds like you know a lot about the northern lights."

"I know some things," I said modestly.

"Could you tell me about them?"

I shrugged. "Sure. The northern lights, properly called the aurora borealis, are the product of the inter-action that happens when solar flares send electrically charged particles that slam into the earth's magnetic field. Although the dancing curtains of light appear close enough to touch, they are actually occurring about one hundred kilometres above the surface of the earth."

"That's all . . . very interesting," Victoria said. "Although it does sound as though it came straight out of a textbook. I was hoping that, instead of a scientific definition, you might know some other things."

"What sort of other things?" I asked.

"I was hoping for a story."

"A story?"

"Maybe a Native creation myth?" she said tentatively.

"So because I'm Native you figure that I must know some myth about the northern lights, is that what you're saying?"

"I did not mean to offend you," she said.

I sat down beside her on the rock. A small tongue of red cut through the green curtain. It did look beautiful. I looked over at Victoria. She was sitting there, eyes wide open, staring up into the night sky. Oh, what the hell.

"Okay."

"Okay what?" she asked.

"I can tell you a story. Just don't expect too much. I'm really not that good at this sort of thing."

"Your grandfather was."

"Yeah, he was a great storyteller and . . . how do you know that?" I asked.

"My father. He has so many fond memories of his time here. He's told me—many times—about the thrill of sitting around a campfire and hearing his guide, your grandfather, tell him stories. He said your grandfather was the best storyteller he'd ever heard in his entire life."

I laughed. "And I'm supposed to compete with that?"

"I didn't mean to—"

"That's okay, no more apologizing. I'll try a story."

I thought about my grandfather and the things he used to say, the way he told stories. There was no way I could duplicate any of that. I'd just have to try to be myself.

"The world—the place where we live—is made of land and sea and sky. The land and sea are surrounded by a deep ditch, sort of like a valley or a—"

"An abyss?" Victoria suggested. "An immense abyss?"

I shrugged. "Who's telling this story?"

"Sorry," she said. "Please go on."

"And the sky is not made of air or gas but of a solid material, an arch that hangs overtop of the land and sea," I continued. "It is solid, except in one place. High in the middle of the dome is a hole. Not large. Not small. Just big enough to allow the spirits to rise up and enter the spirit world."

I remembered the first time I heard my grandfather tell this story. We were sitting together—with my father—around a campfire, looking up at the northern lights. Just like tonight.

"Are you going to go on?" Victoria asked.

I took a deep breath. "And between the sky and the land and sea below there is a path. It is narrow and slick and dangerous, but it is the only way that the spirits can get from the living world to the spirit world. During the days, and even through the long nights of daylight through the summer, the path is brightly lit, and the spirits are able to find their way. But at night, with only the light from the moon and stars, the path is dark, and the journey for the spirits is dangerous. The lights in the sky are the torches of the spirits who have gone on before. They are lighting the path for the new arrivals. And in the light, the spirits still arriving can look up through the hole and see those who are already there.

They are feasting on the best of foods and playing soccer, kicking around the skull of a walrus."

"That's a wonderful story!"

"Thank you," I said. And then I remembered something else my grandfather had said, and the way he had said it. "There's more. Listen."

"Do you hear something?" she whispered anxiously.

"No, no, don't worry . . . it's part of the story."

"Oh, the story," she sighed.

"Listen. Do you hear that sound?" I asked.

"I just hear the fire crackling."

"There's something else besides the fire. Just listen to the sky."

Victoria turned her head so that one ear was aimed skyward.

"Do you hear it now?" I whispered.

"Is it a whistling sound?" she asked hesitantly.

"That's it. Do you know what that sound is?" I asked.

"The noise of the magnetic field being hit by the particles?" she asked.

"Now who's being scientific?"

She smiled. "Please go on."

"The sound is the voices of the spirits in the afterworld. They are calling out, offering encouragement to those coming up the path. They are singing the songs of the elders." I stopped.

"Is that the end?" Victoria asked.

"My grandfather told me that stories are never over," I said. "I'm just going to stop telling it there. Maybe we should try to get to sleep now."

"Will the fire continue to burn through the night?" she asked.

"Will it help you sleep better if you know it will?"

She nodded her head.

"Then I'll make sure it does."

I got up to gather enough deadfall to keep the fire going until morning.

CHAPTER THIRTEEN

I OPENED MY EYES SLIGHTLY and then brought a hand up to shield them from the light. The sun was filtered through the leaves of the trees over my head. A thin column of smoke rose up into the blue, above the trees and high into the sky and—I sat bolt upright as it all came flooding back. Victoria and Andrew were curled up together on the other side of the fire. I jumped to my feet and started kicking dirt onto the fire, trying to erase the trail of smoke.

"What are you doing?" Victoria demanded angrily as she jumped to her feet. I'd showered her and Andrew with dirt as I tried to douse the fire.

"The fire! We can't let them see the smoke!" I practically shouted. "It might show them where we are!"

"Surely there's not enough smoke for anyone to determine our whereabouts," she said.

"We can't take that chance!" I yelled as I finished covering the burning embers and the last few wisps of smoke seeped up. "That's better."

"Do you really think anybody could have seen it?" Victoria asked.

"There wasn't much smoke . . . probably not."

"What time is it?" Andrew asked as he stood up and shook off the dirt.

"It's a few minutes before seven o'clock," Victoria said.

"Seven o'clock!" I exclaimed. "We should have been up and gone an hour ago!"

"We were all so exhausted," Victoria said. "We needed to sleep."

"We needed to get going!" I argued. "We've wasted over two hours of light! Come on, let's move!"

"Can't we get something to eat?" Andrew asked. "I am so famished."

"I've got some berries for you to . . ." I reached my hand into my pocket and pulled out a gooey, inedible mess. I must have rolled over on them in my sleep. "I *had* some berries for you."

"Can we go back and get some more?" Victoria asked.

"We don't have time. We have to get moving in the right direction."

"It's only a few minutes away," Victoria said. "And I'm sure we would be better able to travel today if we had some food."

I hesitated. We did need to get moving, but my stomach was growling as well. There would be more berry patches ahead . . . most likely.

"Please. We won't take long."

"I guess it would be okay."

"Thank you," Victoria said.

"Yes, thank you," Andrew echoed.

"But we have to make up the lost time . . . all the time we lost by sleeping. We'll be moving double time for the entire day until we reach the fishing lodge."

"We'll keep whatever pace you set, you have our word on that," Victoria said.

"Then come on."

We started back down the slope toward the berry patch. It was only a couple of hundred metres away, but I hated the idea of starting the day heading in the wrong direction. Each step down the path was one more step we'd have to retrace to get back to where we'd started.

"Do you think we can make it to the fishing lodge today?" Victoria asked.

"If we'd gotten up and started moving two hours ago we'd have had a good chance. Now?" I said with a shrug. "I'm not so sure."

"I do not want to spend another night in the forest," Andrew said. It sounded more like a command than an opinion.

"We can't afford to spend another night," I said. "We have to get to the lodge so we can get some help for Ray and Albert."

"Do you think . . . do you think that they are—"

"They're all right," I said, cutting her off. "I'm sure of that."

"How can you be so certain?"

"I was thinking about it. Thinking about it a lot. They're still okay."

"Why would you believe that . . . especially after what they did to poor Nigel?" she asked.

"That was different."

"How?" Andrew asked. "How was that different?"

"Nigel was . . . was . . . well, what happened to him happened at the beginning. Probably when they first came in. Both sides might have been shooting. He was probably killed when they tried to capture everybody. They've already captured Ray and Albert, so they aren't a threat."

"That seems logical," Victoria said hesitantly.

"If they were going to kill them they would have done it right away. Maybe they figure if they can't capture you two then at least they have somebody. Doesn't that make sense?"

"These people seldom make sense."

I stopped and grabbed her by the arm. "These people? Do you know who they are?"

She shook her head. "Extremists of some type. Violence for one cause or another."

"Sometimes people get desperate," I said.

"My goodness, it sounds as though you are defending their actions!" Victoria snapped.

"Of course not. I'm just saying that sometimes people have things taken away from them—important things—and they're angry and bitter because, no matter what they do, they know they can't get back what belongs to them."

Victoria looked confused and hurt.

"Look, I'm not saying that any of this is right, but I understand . . . I'm Native. Lots of Natives are angry."

"People in your village?" Victoria asked.

"Sure . . . some, I guess."

"Then that would explain it."

"Explain what?"

"How those men knew my brother and I were here."

"What do you mean?"

"Somebody in your village must have tipped them off," she said.

"The only two people in the village who know who you are are my father and grandmother. Are you saying that one of them is responsible?" I asked in shock.

"Not them directly, but they must have told somebody who told somebody else, and so forth."

"You're nuts!" This was going too far, and I was getting really angry.

"You cannot talk to my sister in that tone!" Andrew snapped.

"Shut up, you little twerp, or I'll *make* you shut up!" I said as I took a step toward him.

"You would not dare lay a finger upon him!"

"Then you'd both better shut up! First off, my grandmother and my father wouldn't have said a word to anybody! Second, even if they did, how do you figure that those people could have gotten here that fast?"

"Well . . ."

"Think about it!" I demanded. "It was less than thirty-six hours between the time you first showed up in our village and the time those men took over our camp. Somebody talked when they shouldn't have, but it happened before you even appeared in our village! It was somebody outside . . . somebody involved with you!"

"That is not possible."

"Nothing else makes sense, and—" I stopped in shock. A flash of colour caught my eye, and then I saw a man emerge from the trees! Thank goodness he wasn't close. He had to be at least about a hundred metres away. Then a second and third man appeared. I grabbed Victoria with one hand and Andrew with the other and pulled them down to the ground.

"Unhand us this instant or—"

"Shut up and be quiet!" I hissed at Victoria. "Didn't you see them?"

"See them? See who?" she whispered.

"Three men. They're coming up the slope, following right behind us."

"Did they see us?" she asked.

"I don't think so."

I crawled forward into the cover of a bush. Andrew and Victoria followed behind. I pushed myself forward until I could look through the cover but remain hidden.

"I can't see them," Victoria said.

"Neither can I now."

"Are you sure that you saw somebody?" Andrew asked.

"Of course I'm sure—there they are!"

Three men were working their way up the slope. They were holding weapons—rifles—and carrying packs on their backs. They were moving slowly in our direction.

"Are they . . . are they the men who are after us?" Victoria whispered.

"Who else could it be?"

"Maybe it's somebody coming to rescue us," Andrew suggested.

"Not likely. Who even knows you need to be rescued?"

"If Albert got free, then—"

"There were four men with weapons and he and Ray were tied up," I said. "They weren't getting away. And even if they did, how could they get help so fast?"

As we watched, the three men stopped. They seemed to be studying something.

"We have to get out of here," I said. "Come on."

I started to move back up when I suddenly realized that just above us the entire slope was open and exposed. If we went that way we'd be seen for sure. I changed directions. We had to stop going up and head across the face of the slope, staying in the cover of the trees and bushes. Victoria and Andrew were tucked in right behind me. I had to fight the urge to run. We had to move quietly . . . slowly . . . staying out of sight. We started forward. As the slope increased, I dropped down on my bottom and slid down the hill. Victoria and Andrew came down right behind me, bumping into me when the hill flattened out. I tried to stand up but my legs felt all shaky and I tumbled back down to the ground.

"We'll stop here," I said. "We're safe . . . at least for a minute."

"How did they know how to find us?" Victoria asked.

"I don't know for sure. Maybe they saw the smoke from the fire. Maybe they were just tracking us, following our trail."

"Is that really possible?"

"Some of my uncles can track a bear that way. We weren't being careful, we probably left a trail that was pretty easy to follow."

"So what do we do now?" Victoria asked.

"We do what we were going to do. We have to keep going. We have to get to the fishing lodge."

"Are we still headed in the right direction?"

"We're not exactly going the way I wanted, but we're not going in the wrong direction. We're just swinging off to the side. As soon as we put some more distance between us and them I'll try to get us back on a more direct route."

"Does that mean that we are not going to arrive tonight?" Victoria asked.

"I don't know. We're going a longer way, but I plan to be moving faster." I stood up and started walking again.

I looked back. Andrew and Victoria were following, side by side, her arm around his shoulder. I could see that he was crying. I couldn't blame him. I was fighting hard to keep my emotions in check. The only chance we had was for me to stay focused, to stay in charge, to . . . I felt tears start to flow down my face. I couldn't let them see that. I bit down on the inside of my cheek and wiped away the tears with the back of my hand. I stepped up my pace and kept my face hidden from them.

Our path crossed a rocky creek bed. There was only a trickle of water running along the stony course. I bent down and cupped a handful of water, splashing it on my face, washing away any trace of the tears. I cupped them again and brought my hands up to my mouth. The water was cold and tasted as good to me as those berries had the night before.

I looked up at Victoria and Andrew. They both looked scared and shaken.

"Get a good drink. We're going to be going hard for a long time."

"Will they be able to catch us?" Victoria asked.

"Not as long as we keep moving. Tracking isn't fast. We should be able to stay ahead of them. Come on, we're going to head down this creek bed."

"But shouldn't we be heading up?" Victoria said.

"If they follow us here they'll expect us to climb. They'll waste a lot of time going up, looking for where we leave the rocks. By doubling back, heading down, we can gain some time."

"That seems . . . wise."

"Try and stay on the big rocks as we travel. That way there's no trail left behind."

I bounded from rock to rock, and they did the same behind me.

"At least we know that Ray and Albert are still okay," I said.

"We do?" Victoria asked.

"Definitely. There were only three men on our trail."

"So?"

"The fourth must be back at the camp with them. If they'd done something to Ray and Albert they wouldn't have needed to leave somebody behind. Doesn't that make sense?"

"Yes . . . yes, it does. I am afraid that I'm not think-ing very clearly," she said.

"I know what you mean," I said.

"You do?" she asked. "You have been so calm. So in control."

"Me?"

"Yes. Without you, I don't know what we would have done."

Obviously she hadn't seen the tears or the shaking.

"I am so sorry for the things I said. I know your family is not responsible. Please accept my apologies and my thanks."

"The apologies I'll accept. The thanks had better wait."

CHAPTER FOURTEEN

"OKAY, WE'LL TAKE A SHORT BREAK," I said.

Victoria had her arm around Andrew and she tried to ease him to the ground. He seemed to collapse. His face was blank and he just stared into space.

"I'm going to go a little bit farther—scout to the top of the hill," I said. Victoria looked worried. "I'll be right back, don't worry. Just rest and take care of your brother."

She gave me a faint smile and nodded her head ever so slightly. "He needs something to eat."

"Well, we all do. Maybe there'll be some more berries." We'd passed through a couple of patches earlier in the day and grabbed berries as we'd walked.

"We need more than berries," she said.

"We haven't passed any cheeseburger patches!" I snapped.

"But what about other things? Don't people live off the land?"

"Some people. People with a rifle and fishing rod and traps maybe."

"In one of the books I was reading there was mention of edible roots and—"

"I don't want to hear about what you've read in a book because . . ." I stopped myself, remembering that she'd been able to start a fire. "Actually, anything you can remember would be good . . . I'm hungry too."

Her smile grew wider. She really was very pretty. Seemed to me she looked a lot like her mother.

"I'll be back in a few minutes."

I slowly worked my way up the slope. The incline was taking a toll on my legs. They were aching and tired. We'd been pushing hard all day. I didn't have a watch and I hadn't asked Victoria the time for hours. The last time I'd checked it was five o'clock. Suppertime.

It didn't help that the route I'd chosen wasn't the most direct or the easiest. I'd deliberately taken us along paths that would be harder to track—creek beds, hardened dirt and rocky ways. Three times I'd even reversed our route and doubled back. Once I did it to throw them off our trail. The other two times were because I made a wrong turn. I didn't say that to Victoria or Andrew. They didn't need to know everything.

Besides, it wasn't that much farther. I figured that from the top of this hill I should be able to see the lodge, or at least the tip of its radio antenna sitting up above the trees. I knew Andrew didn't have much more in him. Heck, I didn't have much left myself. We were all running on empty—empty stomachs.

The hill started to flatten out. At the same time, the trees and bushes were becoming smaller as they became exposed to the north winds that raced over the top of the hill. I reached the crest. The lodge would be just on the edge of a small inlet. But there was no lodge . . . there wasn't even an inlet. The lake stretched out before me to the horizon. Had we overshot it, or had I overestimated how far we'd travelled because of all the twists and turns?

I slumped to the ground. What were we going to do now? What was I going to say to Andrew and Victoria? Which direction were we going to go? I didn't know the answers to any of those questions. What I did know was that I had to get back to where they were resting.

I trotted down the slope, the incline encouraging my weakened legs to go faster. I skidded to a stop. Andrew and Victoria were rushing up toward me.

"What's wrong?" I demanded, although I was certain I already knew the answer.

"They're coming!" Victoria exclaimed.

"You saw them?"

"We caught a glimpse of them through a gap in the trees."

"How far away?"

"I don't know. They were just tiny. Maybe far."

"Did they see you?" I demanded.

"No."

"Come on," I said. "We've got to get going. Let's go this—"

"No!" Victoria said, grabbing me by the arm and spinning me around. "That's the direction they're coming from!"

"That can't be!" I exclaimed. "We came from the other direction."

"I know what I saw. They're coming from over there," she said, waving her arm and pointing.

"But we came from the other direction. How can they be tracking us if they aren't following our trail?" I demanded. "Maybe they've lost our tracks."

"No. They were heading straight for us," she said.

I paused. I needed to be certain. "You're *sure* they're that way?" I asked.

"I am completely positive."

"Okay, come on, we'll go this way and—"

I stopped as Andrew slumped to the ground.

"What are you doing?"

He didn't answer.

"Get up!" I said as I reached down and grabbed him by the arm.

"Leave me alone!" he snapped as he shook off my hand.

"We have to get going!"

"I am not going anywhere," he said. "What's the point?"

"The point is, if we stay here they're going to get us."

"They are going to get us anyway," he said.

"They're *not* going to get us," I argued, trying to sound convincing.

"Of course they are. They have tracked us this far. They have weapons and supplies—food. And with each passing hour, as we get weaker, they remain stronger. They are going to catch us."

"Fine, then you stay here! Sit right here. Wave to them for all I care. Maybe after they've caught you they'll be satisfied and go back. Or maybe having you with them will slow them down, the way you've slowed us down, and your sister and I will get away! Come on, Victoria," I said, and I started off.

I took a few steps before I realized that Victoria wasn't coming with me. She was standing beside Andrew.

"I cannot leave him," she said.

I hadn't really intended to leave him behind. I was bluffing. I figured if the two of us started to walk away he would come after us.

"They are not after you," Victoria said. "There is nothing you can do to help us. Please save yourself. I understand."

She was right. They weren't after me. Once they got the two of them they wouldn't waste another second coming for me. I had to fight the urge to simply leave. I couldn't. I walked back to them.

"I guess we are wasting our time. We don't have a chance," I said.

Andrew nodded his head slowly.

"Of course, it would be different if it weren't for you guys. If I were with a couple of my cousins we could get away—easy." I paused. "But I shouldn't have expected anything more from the two of you." I laughed. "Imagine me thinking a couple of spoiled rotten little *royals* who've been catered to and pampered their whole lives could ever show enough guts. It's like they say, when the going gets tough, the tough get—"

"That's not fair!" Victoria snapped. She grabbed Andrew roughly by the arm and pulled him to his feet.

"You get going! Now!" she shouted as she pushed him in the right direction.

I tried to keep the smile off my face.

"And *you* were fooling nobody with that little speech of yours!" she muttered.

"I don't know what you mean," I lied. "No idea whatsoever."

I stopped and tried to figure out which way to go. I knew where the lake was. That would be hard to lose. I just didn't know where we were on the lake. If we'd overshot the fishing lodge, there was nothing for another hundred kilometres. I didn't know where we were—we were lost. Lost. I tried to remember what advice I'd been given, what you should do when you're lost.

"It will be all right. We just have to stay ahead of them," Victoria said.

"That's not enough. If they don't get us, then the wilderness will."

"We will be fine."

"Look, Victoria, I haven't wanted to say anything. I didn't want to worry you and your brother. But I have to be honest."

"We're lost," she said. "You have no idea where we are."

"I have *some* idea. How long have you known?"

"A while," she said.

"I know what I'm supposed to do," I said. "I just can't do it."

"Why not?"

"You're either supposed to stay put so you don't get more lost, or, if you can, retrace your steps back to where you started. We can't do either. It might be better if I had a compass."

"A compass? I don't have a compass, but I do have a way to tell directions."

"Let me guess, you're going to look for moss growing on the north side of trees."

"Not exactly, but I can tell which direction is south," she said.

"How?"

"Like this." She held her arm up in the air, studied the back of her hand, then the sky. "South is that way," she said.

"What makes you think that? Is it written on your hand?" I asked sarcastically.

"I was not looking at my hand, I was looking at my watch."

"Your watch has a compass built into it?"

"No, but I read about a way to make your watch into a compass. You simply aim the hour hand directly at the sun, and south is halfway between the direction the hand is pointing to and the twelve."

"Are you joking around?" I asked.

"No. That way is south."

I was going to argue, but actually that was the direction I thought was south. She'd been right about the way to start a fire. Maybe she was right about this as well.

"That helps, but still, I wish we could just retrace our steps."

"But since we can't, we will have to keep going forward. In three days, when we do not appear as scheduled, a search party will be sent. They will find us."

"You make it sound easy. Do you have any idea how hard it is to find somebody who's missing up here, especially when they're not where they're supposed to be?" I asked.

My father had been involved with a number of search and rescue operations. I'd even gone along on a couple. It's a big, big country.

"They *will* find us," she said. "That is a certainty."

How could she be so positive? "Victoria . . . is there something you're not telling me about?"

She smiled. "Andrew and I are both carrying personal locating devices."

"What?"

"It's called a Lotex," Victoria said. She reached into her pocket and pulled out a small object about the size of a little flashlight, with a long wire tail attached.

"This is a radio transmitter, powered by two small batteries. Our signal is bounced off a satellite and the receiver uses a global positioning system to determine our location to within a few metres, anywhere in the world."

"And you both have these?" I asked.

"We carry them with us whenever and wherever we travel," she explained.

"Everywhere?"

"Everywhere," she confirmed.

My head was spinning. "And . . . and . . . do people know this?"

"Of course, the members of the royal entourage and our security detail and—"

"But other people! Do other people know you carry these things?"

"It is fairly standard procedure. I would imagine that many people would be aware of this practice," she admitted.

"Give me your transmitter."

Victoria handed it to me.

"Both of you!" I snapped. "Right now!"

Andrew stood up and dug his out of his pocket and handed it to me.

"And the thing that gets your signals . . . the . . . the . . ."

"The receiver?" she asked.

"Yeah, the receiver. How big is it?"

"Larger than the transmitter, of course, but not very large."

"Small enough to fit in a plane?" I asked.

"Oh, goodness! Much smaller."

"Could it fit in a backpack?"

"Certainly, and . . . what are you saying?" Victoria asked.

"We have to get rid of these things," I said, holding up the tracking devices.

"We cannot do that!" She reached over and tried to take them from me, but I pulled them away.

"Don't you see? These are how they're tracking us,

how they know where we are! Don't you understand?"

"That cannot be. What you do not *understand* is that each of these transmitters has a different signature to identify who is carrying it. Only those with the highest clearance among palace security would know our codes."

"*You* don't understand. Nobody has to know your codes. Look around! How many of these little transmitters do you think are out here? All they have to do is follow the only two signals that are being sent out! Yours," I said, pointing to her. "And yours," I said to Andrew. "We have to destroy them."

"Destroy them?" Victoria asked anxiously.

"Yeah. Let's smash them, and—"

"They are very durable," she said.

"We'll see how durable they are when I hit them with a rock," I said.

"You can try, but it won't harm them."

"We'll see." I put them both down on the ground and picked up a large rock. I lifted it over my head and threw it down to the ground. There was a loud crash.

"We'll see how durable they . . ." I picked them up. There wasn't so much as a dint or a scratch on the cases.

"They are meant to remain functional even in the event in an airplane accident," Victoria said.

"Come on, there's no way it could survive a plane crash."

Victoria and Andrew didn't answer, but they looked at each other, and I knew that what she had said was true, and they knew it because their mother had been carrying one when her plane went down. I felt awful.

"Okay, if I can't smash them, maybe we can drown them. Let's drop them in the lake."

"They are also waterproof. They transmit even if they're underwater."

"Then I guess we'll just have to leave them behind. At least they won't be able to track us any more. I just wish there was something else that . . . wait a minute . . . I've got an idea."

CHAPTER FIFTEEN

I TIED THE TWO LOCATORS around the piece of driftwood, using their long wire tails. I secured the knots and then doubled them up. Gently I pushed the piece of wood into the river. It drifted and spun slowly, heading toward the very centre, and then it was captured by the current. It picked up speed as it bobbed away.

"Jamie, do you think this will work?" Victoria asked.

"Don't know. What I do know is that we won't have long to wait to find out. Come on."

I started to wade across the water.

"What are you doing?" Victoria asked.

"Trying not to leave tracks."

"But you said they were tracking us through the transmitters." She sounded a bit confused.

"I'm pretty sure that's how they're doing it, but we can't take any chances. We'll walk upstream a few hundred metres, look for some rocks that will cover our tracks when we leave the water, and then we're going to head up to the top of that cliff," I said, pointing upstream.

"Do we have to climb that?" Andrew asked.

"I want to get someplace where we can see them, but hopefully they can't see us."

I continued upstream, and Victoria and Andrew trailed after me.

"Be careful, it's a little slippery in spots," I warned them.

The river was cold, but the cold felt good. I cupped some water and brought it up to my lips. It felt great as it slid down my throat. Now all I needed was some food. And a soft bed, and ten hours of sleep . . . and my father to come and take us to safety. He'd know what to do if he were here.

"Walk right where I walk," I said, as I stepped out of the water and onto a large rock. "Remember, no tracks."

I stepped on another stone, balancing myself. Then another stone, and another. The last one rocked underfoot, threatening to buck me off. I stepped to the side and offered a hand, first to Andrew and then to Victoria, as they came to the teetering rock. They reached the end of the stones and took a few steps across some soft sand before they reached the rocks and debris at the bottom of the cliff. I followed behind them, walking backwards, bending down and using my hands to brush away the indentations that marked our steps.

"Do we really have to climb this?" Victoria asked.

I looked straight up the cliff face. It certainly looked a lot steeper up close than it had from a distance.

"We'll walk along the base until we see an easier way up," I suggested.

Andrew was already ahead of me. I was amazed, but he seemed to be in much better shape than he'd been a few hours earlier. Somehow he must have gotten a second wind.

"How about here?" he asked.

There was a seam, a sort of small gully, stretching down from the top of the cliff. It was covered in loose rock, but it did look possible to climb.

I started to scramble up, bending forward and using my hands to help steady me. A few of the rocks slipped beneath my feet, but not enough to stop me from moving forward. I reached the top and practically toppled over. I spun around and offered a hand to the others.

"Thank you. That was more of a climb than I had anticipated," Victoria said.

We were fairly high up now, and we had a good view up and down the river for hundreds and hundreds of metres. We were sheltered from view by the rim of the cliff. Behind us, trees and bushes offered enough cover that we could slip into the forest without being seen if necessary.

"As long as we stay low to the ground we have the perfect place to see, but not be seen," I said.

"Is this low enough?" Andrew asked as he flopped to the ground.

"Just about perfect," I said.

He rolled onto his back and closed his eyes.

"Do you think we'll have long to wait?" Victoria asked.

"I don't know for sure, but I doubt it. They've never been very far behind. Why don't you follow Andrew's lead and close your eyes, try to get some sleep."

"I was thinking that perhaps I could find some food," she said.

"Food?" Andrew asked, suddenly opening his eyes.

"I could go into the forest and search for something edible. There are roots and tubers that I've read about. I just wish I had some sort of digging tool."

"Would a knife help?" I asked.

"Yes, that would be excellent!"

I reached into my back pocket, pulled out my Swiss Army knife and handed it to her.

"Hopefully I'll be back soon," she said, and she started off for the woods.

"Don't go far," I warned her. "The last thing I need is for you to get lost."

"I will stay close by."

"Should I go with her?" Andrew asked.

I shook my head. "You should just stay here. Rest." I settled in on my belly beside him. It felt so good just to lie there. It would have been so easy to fall asleep. It had been so long since I'd slept. So long since I'd eaten. My mind started to fill up with the image of my bedroom. My bed. My covers and pillow and—I felt myself drifting off, so I pushed myself up. I had to fight the urge to close my eyes. It was important that I keep watch. Somebody had to look out for us.

"Jamie?"

I looked over at Andrew. I was surprised he was awake.

"Jamie . . . are we going to be all right?"

"We've been all right so far."

"I mean, is this going to work? Are they going to chase the transmitters?"

"I hope so."

"And if they don't?"

"Then we keep moving. We keep away from them."

"How long before we get to the fishing lodge?"

"We're not going to the fishing lodge," I told him.

"But why not?"

I took a deep breath. I wasn't about to tell him that I didn't even know how to find it. "Lots of reasons, but mainly because I'm afraid that we won't be safe there."

"Why not?"

"These people aren't stupid. The fishing lodge is the only thing in this direction. They must have figured out that's what we were headed for."

"Then why did we even bother going this way?" he demanded. "Why did you lead us in this direction?"

"Because at first we didn't know they could track us. We figured they didn't even know which direction we were heading."

"So what are we going to do?"

"We're going to backtrack. Go in the opposite direction."

"We're going back to the camp?"

"We're going back in the direction of the camp. We're going back to my village."

"That'll take us days!"

"I think about four days."

"We can't go another four days without food!" he exclaimed.

"We won't have to." Victoria was walking toward us, holding something in her hands.

"What are those?" Andrew asked.

"Roots. I cannot guarantee the taste or tenderness, but from what I've read I know that they are edible."

She sat down as both Andrew and I sat up. She handed us each a piece of the root. It was mostly white, with brown—dirt—covering some of it. It reminded me of a potato, sort of a long, thin potato. I brushed it against my shirt, trying to remove as much dirt as possible. Then I sank my teeth in and took a small bite. It was softer than I had expected. The taste was . . . well, it was like chewing on soft, wet chalk. Somehow I'd expected whatever I ate to taste wonderful, the way water is so good when you're really thirsty. Wrong. I swallowed anyway.

"Not exactly gourmet fare," Victoria said.

"I don't know," I said. "Best thing I've eaten in days."

"It's the *only* thing you've eaten in days," she pointed out.

I smiled in response.

"There they are!" Andrew snapped.

I spun around. The three men were only a few hundred metres away, standing by the side of the river.

"Is that where we entered the water?" Victoria asked.

"They're farther downriver," I said. "That means they weren't following our trail."

"Then it *was* the transmitters," Victoria said grimly.

"Let's see what they do. If they go straight downstream then we know for sure."

On cue, the three men turned away from us and began working their way down the river.

"That seals it. If they were tracking they would have had to go both directions to look for where we exited the water. They're following the devices."

We watched as they continued downstream. Finally they disappeared around a bend in the river.

"Now we have to pray for good luck," I said.

"Good luck?"

"We have to hope that the piece of wood stayed in the current and kept going down the river. Hopefully it made it all the way to the lake and is drifting around out there. As long as it's moving, they'll keep following it. Once it stops, they'll catch up fast and realize what we've done."

"So what do we do now?" Victoria asked.

"We give them a few minutes to go farther down the river, and then we head back down the river too."

"We're going to follow them?" Andrew asked in amazement.

"Of course not. When they do find the transmitters they'll come back upriver and try to track us. They'll know we came down to the river to put the things in the water, so they'll look for tracks. I want to use our tracks into the river to cover our tracks out of the river, back to where we came from. We'll walk down the river to that same spot. Are you two ready to go?"

In answer, Victoria and Andrew both got to their feet. I stuffed the two pieces of root that I was holding into my pocket, and they both did the same. That was going to be our bedtime snack.

"Now what I want us to do as we're going back down this cliff is kick up a lot of rocks."

They both looked confused.

"I want it to be obvious to anybody who's coming up the river that this is the spot where we left."

I dropped over the edge of the cliff first. Rocks and dirt showered down ahead of me, and then I was overtaken by other rocks being dislodged from above me by Victoria. I skidded to a stop at the bottom. There was the patch of sand where I'd brushed off our tracks. This time I *wanted* tracks.

"I want you to turn around and walk backwards across this section. I want us to leave prints that look like we came out of the water right here."

I started across, looking over my shoulder as I moved. Victoria and Andrew did the same. I stepped into the water, where my tracks became invisible. I took first Victoria's hand and then Andrew's as they reached the water's edge.

"Now we have to move as fast as we can," I told them.

I fixed my eyes on the river ahead. I hadn't said anything, but this was the most dangerous part of the trip. If those transmitters had travelled no farther than around the bend in the river, then the men would already be heading back. They could be right around the bend, right in front of us. There'd be no place for us to hide. I took a quick look behind me. Andrew and Victoria were falling behind.

"Hurry up!" I demanded of them. "Hurry!"

I turned my attention back downriver. We had less than fifty metres to go to the spot where we'd originally walked into the water. The bend was another two hundred metres beyond that. If they came around the bend now, there was no way they wouldn't see us. Maybe we'd still have a chance to get away . . . unless they shot at us. No, they wouldn't do that, because they wanted to capture Victoria and Andrew, not kill them. At least I was pretty sure they did. Of course that didn't mean they wouldn't shoot at me. If I were one of those guys I'd try to take out the leader. A cold shiver ran up my spine that had absolutely nothing to do with the chilly water I was wading through.

Victoria splashed up beside me. "How long before the sun goes down, before we stop for the night?"

"What time is it now?"

She looked at her watch. "It is almost eleven o'clock."

"Two and a half hours before the sun sets."

"That is a long time," she said.

"We have to get back down the trail as far as we can. As far away from *them* as we can."

"I don't know if Andrew can travel another two and a half hours tonight." She paused. "I do not know if *I* can travel that long."

I didn't feel that strong myself.

"We'll see how far we can get. Let's just get out of the water, and out of sight. Look, here's where we came to the stream the first time."

I waded out of the water and stood on the rocks.

Victoria stumbled and almost fell. I reached out and grabbed her by the hand to help her. I felt embarrassed holding onto her and I quickly released her hand. Andrew was still twenty metres upstream. I was going to yell at him, then I changed my mind. I jumped back into the water and waded back upstream to help.

"You're doing okay. I just want you to do okay a little faster."

"I'm trying."

"Just try a little harder for a little longer. We'll get out of the water and travel a bit farther and then we'll go to sleep." I took him by the arm and urged him along.

"Thank you," he said softly.

We quickly reached Victoria. She was sitting on a rock with her feet dangling in the water. Andrew crawled out of the water and started to sit down beside his sister. I pulled him back to his feet.

"This isn't the time to rest. We're exposed here. You see those trees over there?" I said, pointing to a spot no more than twenty metres away. "You get there and you can rest."

"Come on, Andrew," Victoria said. "I'll take your arm and we'll walk together."

"I can't," he gasped. "Too exhausted."

I felt a sudden rush of anger. I felt like dragging him by the scruff of the neck and . . . but I couldn't do that. It wasn't the way. Besides, I didn't know if I had the strength.

"Andrew," I said softly, "I know you're tired, but we just can't stop right here. All I'm asking you to do is walk to those trees. You can go that far, can't you?"

He looked over. "I . . . think I can."

"Good boy!" I exclaimed. "Let me help you up."

I offered him my hand. Victoria did the same. Together we pulled him to his feet.

"And one more thing," I said. "We all have to walk *backwards*. I want you to walk backwards away from the river. See if you can leave some clear prints that look like they lead into the water."

"Do we have to?" Andrew whined.

"We don't have to do anything if you want to get . . ." I stopped myself. "It would be best."

"How do we even know they'll come across this spot?" Andrew asked.

"That's a good question," Victoria agreed. "Won't they simply continue to track our transmitters down the river and into the lake? That's how they have been tracking us so far, is it not?"

"It is, and they will follow the signals until they find them . . . which could be a day, or hours, or they might have found them already. And once they've found them they'll come looking for us again."

"How do you know they will come looking here?" Victoria asked.

"For a number of reasons. Once they have the transmitters in their hands they'll know we figured it out and it won't work to track us that way. Second, they'll know that we had to get close to the water—upstream of where they found the transmitters—and they'll start working their way up the river to try to find some tracks." I paused. "They could be working their way upriver right now."

Andrew looked long and hard down the river. "I think we should move."

We started out to walk backwards across the soft sand and mud. We certainly couldn't move as fast that way, and it left us visible for a little bit longer to anybody who rounded the bend, but I figured it might just be worth the risk. At the edge of the river we left very visible, very clear footprints. They certainly looked to me like we'd been walking into the water. We kept moving backwards until my feet no longer left impressions on the ground.

"We can turn around now," I said as I spun around.

Both Victoria and Andrew followed my lead. As I looked back at them over my shoulder I stumbled over a rock and almost tumbled to the ground. Victoria reached out and steadied me.

"Are you all right?" she asked.

"Fine . . . thanks . . . just tired."

"My legs feel as though they're filled with lead," she said. "Each step is becoming terribly, terribly difficult."

"I know. But you don't have many more steps to take."

The open ground had given way to waist-high bushes that were becoming more and more frequent. Just beyond that was the edge of the forest.

Suddenly Andrew tripped and fell to the ground. Victoria rushed to his side.

"Let me help you, Andrew, we're almost—"

"I cannot take another step. I need to rest," he said, his voice just above a whisper.

This wasn't where I'd wanted to stop—I'd figured we needed to get into the trees. But then again, we were in cover. As long as we were sitting down, nobody could see us. This wouldn't be the worst place to take a break for a few minutes. Besides, I was too tired to argue with him. Too tired even to think about physically dragging him.

"Let's take a twenty-minute break," I said.

I sat down in the dirt. Victoria took a patch of ground right beside her brother. She pulled out a couple of pieces of root from her pocket.

"Would anybody like some?" she asked.

Andrew took one of the pieces and started to gnaw away at it.

"Jamie?" she asked, offering me the second piece.

I shook my head.

"I washed it off in the water when we were wading along. At least I can assure you that it's free of dirt. And I really think you need to eat."

"Why me?"

"You need to keep your wits about you to continue to lead us," she explained.

"What about you?" I asked. "That's your last piece."

"I can share." She tried to break it in two. It bent, but didn't tear apart.

"Do you want me to try?"

She shook her head. "I know what to do." She took the piece of root and placed one end in her mouth. She then bent it over until it broke in two. She offered me the half that hadn't been between her teeth.

"Thanks," I said as I reached out to take it from her.

As I grabbed it our hands touched and she smiled at me . . . what a wonderful smile . . . soft lush lips and . . . Snap out of it! Quickly, embarrassed, I looked away. With all that had gone on, all that was still going on, how could I even be thinking about stuff like that? There was too much danger. Too much that still had to be done to get us to safety.

We had at least three, probably four days of walking ahead of us. Four days with only berries and some roots to eat. We could do it, but it wasn't going to be easy. Boy, was I going to eat when we finally reached my village. My village . . . that thought gave me a warm feeling. I closed my eyes and thought about what it was going to be like to be home. That would be something, to walk into my village, Victoria and Andrew right there with me. I could just picture my mother and father and grandmother and all my family rushing up to me, giving me hugs and slaps on the back and shaking hands. I'd be like a hero, and everybody would be so grateful for what I did. Victoria would be so grateful that she might even throw her arms around me and give me a big hug and—

"Jamie?"

Startled out of my thoughts, I looked up at Victoria.

"I'm sorry. Were you asleep?" she asked.

"No, just thinking." I was very thankful that she couldn't know what I'd been thinking about.

"Andrew is asleep," she said.

He was lying on the ground, his head in her lap, mouth wide open, eyes closed.

"I was wondering, are you positive it is best for us to backtrack along our route?"

"Definitely."

"But to retrace our steps will take us two days," she said. "How many days farther is your village from that point?"

"If we move quickly it's another two days."

"We're not able to move very quickly though, are we?"

"We'll do okay," I offered.

"But what if they're waiting there for us?" she asked.

"At my village?"

She nodded.

"They'd have to be crazy to do that," I said.

"They would?"

"Think about it. Everybody in the whole village, and I mean *everybody*, is related to me. Do you think that my grandmother is going to let anything happen to me . . . or to you?"

"I am certain she would try to stop them, but she is an elderly woman, and they have weapons, and—"

"Those guys aren't the only ones with guns. There's nobody over the age of fourteen in my whole village who doesn't own a hunting rifle."

"Even your grandmother?"

"*Especially* my grandmother. She could shoot a playing card out of your hand at twenty metres."

"She must be a fine shot."

"She is, and so is my mother." And then I started thinking about something I'd said and what I wanted to say about it. I took a deep breath.

"Victoria, I just wanted to say I'm sorry, I wasn't thinking about what I said, about the Lotex and the plane crash. . . . I didn't mean anything."

"That's all right, Jamie."

"I've never had anybody close to me die. It must have been hard to lose your mother."

"It was very difficult. It remains difficult," she said. "When most people have a parent die it is a private tragedy and then life goes on. For me, I get almost daily reminders about my mother. People are always asking me questions or they have pictures of her or—"

"I'm sorry, I didn't mean to bring it up."

"You had reason to bring it up. Others do not, although I know they mean no harm. Her death touched so many people. Did you know she was the most photographed person in the world?"

"She was?"

"Definitely. And she will always be remembered as one of the most beautiful women in the world. Do you know how hard it is to be the daughter of someone that beautiful? No matter what you do, you can never live up to that."

I wanted to say something to her, to tell her that I thought she was really good-looking, but the words stayed in my head and wouldn't come out.

"And just my luck, I have two parents and I have to look like my father instead of my mother. Believe me, I love my father dearly, but one has to admit that he is not the most handsome man in the world. Thank goodness, at least I don't have his ears."

I looked down at Andrew and his jumbo-sized ears.

"Yes, Andrew inherited the family curse," she chuckled. "Look at me now, looking like a complete mess!"

She still looked pretty to me.

"How could I ever compete with the title of most photographed, most beautiful woman in the world? I remember once when she—"

"Over here!" a voice hollered, and we both froze.

CHAPTER SIXTEEN

I STARED WIDE-EYED AT VICTORIA. She looked panicked . . . scared . . . petrified. Andrew slept on, unaware.

"Slowly . . . quietly," I whispered, "flatten yourself to the ground."

She slid down farther, lower, while still keeping Andrew's head on her lap. His eyes remained closed. Maybe it was a good thing he was still asleep.

Just as slowly, I dropped to my belly and began to slither forward.

"What are you doing?" Victoria questioned.

"I have to take a look."

I crawled toward the wall of bushes that was shielding us from the river, protecting us from being seen. Still hidden, I started to poke my head through the branches and leaves until I could just peek out. They were no more than twenty metres away! Involuntarily I ducked back down. They were right there! Silently I took a deep breath and tried to calm myself down. My heart was racing like I'd just run up a long flight of stairs. Slowly, deliberately, against every instinct yelling out that I should just stay hidden, I started to peek out at them again.

There were two men. They wore outdoor clothing and carried big backpacks. Each held a rifle. One was standing while the other was on his knees. They were right where we'd gone into—and come back out of—the river. I knew that the man on his knees was examining our tracks.

"Come!" he yelled out, and then I caught sight of the third man, on the far side of the river. I watched, transfixed, as he started across the water and came right toward them—right toward me! He was looking straight at me, looking at him. Had he seen me? He stopped beside the other two and dropped to his knees to look at the tracks. I felt a rush of relief.

I tried to think what would happen next. There were only two possibilities. One was that they'd be fooled and they'd start going back upstream, looking for the place where we'd left the water. If they did that, we'd be safe, not just for now but maybe altogether. Then I thought about the other possibility. What if they came this way? We were no more than twenty metres from them and there wasn't enough cover to hide us if they got close. We could try to make a break for it, but how far could we possibly get? They had guns, and even if they didn't they could still run us down. Those backpacks were probably filled with food. They'd been eating and keeping strong while we'd been getting weaker and weaker. There was no way we could outrun them. On the bright side, if they caught us they'd probably give us some food.

Suddenly the two men who had been bent over rose to their feet. Whatever was going to happen was going to happen right now. One man splashed back into the water and the other two started to move upriver. They were moving away! They weren't coming for us!

I dropped back down to my belly and scurried over to Victoria and Andrew.

"Well?" Victoria whispered.

"They're there. All three of them. By the river."

"And? Are they coming?" Her voice was barely audible.

I shook my head. "They're going upriver like I thought they—"

Without warning she reached over and threw her arms around me. She pressed her face into my shoulder and . . . what was she doing? And then I felt her shaking and could make out the very faint sound of her sobbing.

"It's okay . . . it's okay," I whispered. Awkwardly I patted her back. "It's okay."

She released her grip on me, and I felt both relieved and disappointed all at once. She used the back of her hand to wipe at her eyes and her nose.

"I am so sorry," she sniffled.

"That's okay."

"I know I have to be strong. I was just so afraid . . . I'm still afraid."

"There's no reason to be afraid now," I said, and then I realized that was a lie. "There isn't *as much* reason to be afraid. They're going away. They're working their way upriver and away from us."

"Oh, Jamie, thank you so much for everything. What do we do now?"

"We let them get farther away. We'll stay here until I see them climb up that cliff and disappear into the forest."

"And then?" she asked.

"And then we crawl to the forest and put some distance between us and them."

"But what will happen when they realize that the trail ends at the forest's edge?" she asked.

"They'll figure that we went that way and they'll start in looking for more tracks."

"And when they don't find any?" she asked.

"Then they'll figure that we're still aiming for the fishing lodge, and that's where they'll go."

"Are you sure?" she asked.

"I'm sure. Now you just rest. I'll watch them move upriver, and as soon as it's clear we'll start walking."

"Will we go very much farther tonight?" she asked.

"Can't. It'll be dark in less than an hour. I can't risk us losing our trail, so we'll stop for the night shortly. I just need us to get into the forest."

"I don't think that Andrew can go much farther tonight," she said.

"I don't think any of us has much left. You close your eyes, get some rest. I'll tell you when it's time to move."

The sun was still low. Once we'd made it into the forest we'd stopped for the night. Victoria had been too tired even to ask about starting a fire. That was good. Even though I'd wanted one, it would have been too risky. It was better to stay hidden and cold, than warm and exposed. After that I'd slept fitfully, closing my eyes enough to rest, but still aware of all the sounds in the forest around us.

Now it was time to go. Every minute that we waited was one more minute before we got to safety. One more minute before we could send back somebody to help Ray and Albert. With everything that had happened my thoughts had been on us and not on them. I could only hope that they were still okay. They had to be okay. There was no reason to hurt either of them. It wasn't like they were still protecting Victoria and Andrew or stopping them from being captured. That was me doing that. Me standing in their way.

I got up and stretched. Instinctively and anxiously I looked down the path in the direction we'd just come. There was, of course, nothing to see but trees. Ahead of us was the path we had travelled once before. I'd been nervous that I'd have trouble retracing our steps. I didn't need to be. The men, in their haste to chase us, had left the vegetation beaten down by their big boots, branches broken off by their clumsy bodies. I think even Andrew could have followed this trail.

I looked down at the two of them sleeping. Curled up together, they both looked so peaceful, as if they didn't have a worry in the world. I was almost tempted to just let them sleep for a little while longer. Tempted, but I really couldn't . . . unless it was still really early. I knew the sun was up there somewhere—probably just creeping over the horizon. I hadn't figured on leaving until around six. I wondered what time it was. If only I had a watch.

Victoria's watch was on her left wrist. Unfortunately, the way she was sleeping, her left wrist was all tucked up underneath her other hand. I got closer and bent down, trying to somehow catch a glimpse of the time. All I could see was the watchband. Maybe if I could just move that one hand slightly I could see. Slowly, carefully, I reached down and took her hand. Her skin was so soft—amazingly soft. Gently I started to move her hand and—

"What are you doing?" she asked groggily.

I dropped her hand and jumped backwards. "I was just trying to find out the time!" I exclaimed. "I'm sorry!"

"Is it time to get up?" Andrew asked as he opened his eyes.

"I don't know," I said. "I don't know what time it is."

Victoria looked at her watch. "It is a few minutes before six."

"Then you could stay asleep for a little bit longer. Maybe ten or fifteen minutes."

"Not likely," Andrew said. "I am awake now, and I have to relieve myself."

He sat up and then slowly got to his feet, stretching and shaking out the kinks in his back and legs as he rose.

"How are you feeling?" Victoria asked him.

"Surprisingly, not too bad," he said. "Rested, more than a bit hungry, but my legs feel good." He lifted first one leg and then the other, pumping them up and down. "I am certain I can travel well today." He paused. "Now if you will both excuse me I need to find the nearest bush."

"Please stay close!" Victoria called after him. "I don't really want you out of my sight!"

He stopped and turned around. "Dear sister, I won't go far, but this is one activity that is best completed out of your sight!"

I burst out laughing and Andrew's face broke into a smile. He turned back around and continued a little way into the forest. Victoria watched him walk away.

"There is more to him than what shows on the surface," she said.

"I never said there wasn't," I said, although I'd certainly been thinking it.

"Actually, Jamie, I believe I was almost talking more to myself than to you. He's demonstrated more intestinal fortitude—guts—than I thought he had."

"He's hung in there pretty good," I agreed. "But so have you."

"Please," she scoffed. "I could have been stronger. We have been completely reliant upon you."

"Not completely. It wasn't me who knew how to use a watch as a compass, or start a fire without a match, or dig up those very tasty roots."

She smiled. "Perhaps I have provided some morsels of information. But you have been the leader."

"I'm supposed to be the leader. I'm the intrepid Native guide, remember?"

"Still, I'm sure this isn't exactly what you anticipated."

I laughed. "That's for sure," I agreed. "None of this is what I expected. *You're* not even what I expected."

"Me?" she asked. "Have I failed to meet your expectations?"

"Not failed. You're just different than I thought you were going to be."

"Go on," she said.

"Well . . . I was just . . . sort of expecting you to act . . . to act more like . . . I don't know."

"It is fine for you to say what you are thinking."

"I just can't put it into words, that's all."

"Allow me," she said. "You had a belief that I would act like some sort of princess. Correct?"

I nodded my head slightly.

"And just how many princesses have you had on these trips?" she asked.

"Well, none, officially, but I've met enough rich people who act like they're royalty," I joked.

"I see. So did you expect me to act all prim and proper? Like some spoiled little prima donna who would demand to be carried about and waited on hand and foot? Is that what you expected?"

"That may be what I expected but—"

"That is nothing but some ridiculous stereotype and it's very offensive to who I am as a person."

"—but you're different," I said, finally finishing my sentence.

She stopped, and her face took on a thoughtful look, like she was actually going to listen. I took a deep breath. And then I took another second to think, to make sure my words were going to come out right.

"Yes, different," I repeated. "You're almost like a normal girl."

"Almost like a normal girl!" she exclaimed. "And what exactly does that mean? That part of me is abnormal? That I am some sort of circus freak?"

"No, of course not!" I protested. "Look, I'm not trying to insult you."

"So far that isn't working!"

"I'm even trying to compliment you!"

"Compliment?" she asked.

I shook my head. "I know that you're not like the girls from around here, the girls that go to my school."

"Go on," she said.

"But except for some of the words you use, and that accent of yours—"

"Are you going to start in about my accent again?"

"No, just let me finish." I paused. "I just think that, except for those things, you could be somebody I go to school with. Somebody I could be friends with." I took a deep breath. Did I have the guts to say what I was really feeling? I took an even deeper breath. "Somebody I could even—"

My words were cut off by a blood-curdling scream—Andrew!

CHAPTER SEVENTEEN

FOR A SPLIT SECOND we were both frozen to the spot, unable to move, or talk, or even think. It was almost as if we'd both heard him cry out but it hadn't really registered. Then his cry came again, this time even louder and more desperate.

"Stay here!" I snapped.

"I am going with you."

"No, it's too dangerous! You have to—"

"He *is* my brother and I *am* going with you!"

There was no time to argue—besides, I wasn't really sure I wanted to go by myself. We both ran.

"Stay behind me!" I barked. I braced myself for whatever we were going to find and wondered what I thought I was going to do. I burst through the bushes and saw . . . nothing. Where was Andrew, and why was he . . . ? Then I saw the bear.

I skidded to a stop and Victoria bumped into me. It was no more than twenty metres away, down the tree-covered slope. It was grey and silver and all hunched over in that way that makes grizzlies seem almost unreal. It wasn't that big—at least for a grizzly. It was probably only about four times as big as I was. It couldn't have been more than a year or so old. It was on all fours, facing away from us, sniffing and snuffling around.

Andrew must have seen it. Maybe his screaming had startled the bear as much as it had us, and in that instant he'd been able to get away. Maybe we could get away too, quietly move back into the bushes and out of its sight. Then we'd circle way around the bear and call out for Andrew. I started to slowly back away, keeping my eyes fixed squarely on the bear.

"Oh my God," Victoria murmured.

"Ssshhh," I whispered to her, "just back away and it won't see us."

"You don't understand . . . it has Andrew."

What did she mean? Surely Andrew had got away. But in that instant I caught sight of him, just a little glimpse of his body, on the ground, partially hidden by a tree, and partially hidden by the bear! I stared, not daring to move. I couldn't help but notice that I wasn't the only person not moving. Andrew was motionless. No movement. No sound. He had to be . . .

"AAAAHHHHHH!" Victoria screamed, and both the bear and I jumped into the air. Before I could react— before I could even think how to react—she started to charge down the slope toward it.

In that split second a hundred different thoughts and feelings and emotions exploded inside my brain. And then I ran after her. I stumbled down the slope, trying to run while keeping my arms held high above my head, trying to convince the bear that I was bigger than it.

The bear rose up on its hind legs and snarled. Victoria skidded to a stop and this time I bumped into her, practically knocking her off her feet. Behind the bear, Andrew lay motionless.

"Leave him alone!" she screamed.

The bear didn't move. It was confused by us—confused enough not to charge—but it wasn't going to retreat and leave its kill behind.

Victoria reached down and grabbed a rock. She threw it at the bear. It hit the ground and bounced wide. She reached down and grabbed another one, much, much larger. There was no way she could toss it that far.

"Give it to me!" I demanded. I took the rock with both hands, lifted it high over my head and heaved it with all my might. It flew through the air but fell short! It bounced and tumbled down the slope and then bashed right into one of the bear's feet.

The bear screeched in pain, jumped into the air, landed on all fours, turned and ran down the hill! It smashed through bushes and snapped off saplings as it charged away. It kept running until it disappeared, the sounds of its escape continuing for a few more seconds after it was lost from sight.

I stood there open-mouthed, not able to believe what had just happened. It was gone. We were safe.

"Andrew," Victoria mumbled.

In my fear and then relief I'd forgotten he was there. Andrew lay still, lifeless, and . . . his pants were down around his ankles. The bear must have ripped them off during the attack. Victoria ran to his side, bent down and threw her arms around him.

"Andrew . . . Andrew . . . Andrew!" she sobbed.

"Is it gone?"

"Andrew?" she exclaimed in disbelief. "You're alive!"

"Of course I'm alive. Now let go of me."

He got up, and as he did he reached down and pulled up his pants.

"You weren't moving . . . you were dead! I mean, I thought you were dead," she sputtered.

"That was the idea," he said. "I wanted the bear to think I was dead so he would leave me alone. Wasn't that smart thinking?"

"It would have been smart if that had been a black bear," I said.

"Whatever do you mean?"

"That was a grizzly. You not moving only made it easier for him. That way he didn't have to catch you before he killed you."

"You mean . . . ?"

I nodded my head. "Grizzlies eat everything, including dead things they find. By the way, what happened to your pants?"

Andrew blushed. "I was sort of taking care of business when the bear appeared. I tried to run but I couldn't move very quickly with my pants down around my ankles. I toppled over." He turned a deeper shade of red.

"The truly important thing is that you're alive!" Victoria exclaimed as she once again threw her arms around him.

"The important thing is that the bear is gone and stays gone," Andrew said. "It *is* gone . . . correct?"

"It's gone, but I don't think we should be sticking around waiting to see if it's coming back. Come on, let's go."

"This looks familiar to me," Victoria said.

"This all looks familiar to me, too," Andrew argued. "Trees, rocks, water. It all looks the same."

"Well we have been here before," Victoria said.

"We have been everywhere before, have we not, Jamie?" he asked.

"We're not lost, if that's what you're worried about."

"I'm not worried . . . not *too* worried." He smiled. "You must admit that I have kept up well today."

"You've done pretty well. We've all done well. We've covered more distance today than any other day. We've put a lot of trail behind us."

"I don't even feel hungry," Andrew said. "At least, not *too* hungry."

We had eaten a ton of blackberries, some more of those roots, and chewed on some leaves that people usually brew to make a tea, but they still tasted pretty good just as they were. We'd passed by an anthill and Victoria had mentioned how she'd read that ants are a good source of protein, but nobody had the guts to be the first to try one to find out.

We came upon a little creek. "Let's stop for a minute and get a drink."

"Will we stop soon for the night?" Victoria asked.

"Not yet. We have at least another hour of light left. Besides, I don't want to stop anywhere near here."

"Why not?" Andrew asked anxiously.

"Do you know where we are?" I asked.

"No . . . where?"

"If we followed this creek downstream we'd come out just by our camp."

"We would?"

"We're no more than two kilometres away."

Andrew suddenly got back to his feet. "We'd better get going . . . we shouldn't be here."

"It's all right," I offered. "There's no reason for them to be looking this way. Besides, the one guy left in the camp probably isn't going to go too far away from Ray and Albert."

"Albert and Ray," Victoria said softly.

"They're fine," I said, guessing what she was thinking. "I'm sure they're fine. They're all tied up, so there's no reason to hurt them."

"And no reason to guard them," Victoria pointed out.

I looked at her. "What do you mean?"

"Since they are securely tied up, perhaps their guard won't judge it necessary to stay at the camp."

"You mean, he might come here?" Andrew asked.

"There's no reason for him to come this way," I repeated.

"But possibly no reason for him to stay there. Perhaps he's flown the plane to the fishing lodge, where he is waiting for us to arrive."

"Maybe," I agreed. "So, what are you getting at?"

"I just thought that perhaps we could go downstream and investigate."

"Investigate?" Andrew asked, sounding more than a little anxious.

"Get close to the camp and just look, to see if—"

"Victoria, you must be insane!" Andrew protested. "We cannot go to the camp! Jamie, tell her we cannot do this!"

They both stared at me.

"I just thought that if they're not being watched, perhaps we could free Ray and Albert. It will be days before we'll reach anybody else who can help them. Going now could make the difference for them. The difference between life and death."

She was right, and I knew it. Even if they were still alive now, that didn't mean they would be alive two or three days from now.

"Still, we cannot go to the camp. It is too dangerous," Andrew said, in that commanding tone he liked to use.

I nodded my head. "He's right. It is too dangerous for us to go to the camp. That's why I'm going alone."

CHAPTER EIGHTEEN

THE FLICKERING OF THE FLAMES from the campfire had been visible for a distance through the trees and brush. This was, at best, a mixed blessing. Obviously it helped guide us to the site, but it also meant that somebody was there tending the fire and guarding Ray and Albert. So much for the faint hope that the person had left.

"This is as close as you two get," I whispered to Victoria and Andrew. We were still a good fifty metres away from the tents, lying on our bellies, hidden by some bushes.

"This is as close as any of us should get," Andrew whispered back in warning. "We know somebody is there. Somebody with a gun. Somebody we should avoid meeting. We should just go."

"We will, but first I need to get a closer look. Don't worry."

"I am well past worried."

"Just stay here, and if anything happens then—"

"If there is no need to worry, I should assume that there is no need to believe that anything will go wrong. If something might go wrong, then I believe I am correct to worry," Andrew said.

"Nothing is going to happen," I said. "But if it does—a one-in-a-million chance—then you two need to know what to do."

"I'm listening," Victoria said.

"Good. You need to go back up the creek. When it gets light, head for the rapids and down to the lake. Follow along the shore. As long as you keep the lake in sight you can't go wrong or get lost. You follow it for two days and you'll come into my village. Guaranteed."

"Or else we will be spotted by the search and rescue parties," Victoria said.

"That's right. We're due back in two days. When we don't show on time they'll almost certainly send somebody out to look for us."

"Not somebody," Andrew said. "Lots of somebodies. You have no idea how the head of our security will react if we are more than a few hours late."

"Even better. Just make sure, before you start waving your arms in the air at a search party, that it isn't the wrong plane, the one with these guys in it," I warned.

"I hadn't even thought about that," Victoria said. "How can we tell?"

"Look before you jump out. Make sure you see the plane before you let it see you. Remember that my father's plane is bright orange, because he'll be part of the search party. Now I have to get going."

I started to get up, but Victoria reached over and grabbed me by the arm. "Please, be careful, Jamie. Please."

"Careful doesn't even begin to describe it," I replied.

She released her grip and I stood. I headed even deeper into the woods. My plan was to circle around to the farthest side of the camp, the place where the trees came closest to the tents. I moved slowly, painfully aware of just how far even a faint noise can travel at night. Just as I thought that, a twig snapped under my foot. I froze in place, not daring to move, hidden within the shadows, not making a sound, listening for anything that might have heard me. There was nothing. Even more carefully I kept going. I could catch more and more flickers of light from the fire as I continued to circle, moving closer.

Finally I came to a spot almost directly behind the tents. The closest tent, the one just in the clearing outside the safety of the trees, the one that held Ray and Albert, was no more than twenty metres in front of me. I focused on the fire. There was nobody sitting by it, but I remembered how they'd previously been hiding in the shadows and appeared only to toss another log onto the fire. Actually, the fire was very low, little more than embers. It had been a long time since a log had been added. Maybe the guard had fallen asleep, leaving the fire to die out. That made sense. Even if somebody was here, he still had to sleep sometime. Sometime like now. He had to be in one of the other tents, sleeping. Maybe I could just—

"Jamie."

I jumped into the air, spun around and fought not to scream. It was Victoria.

"I am so sorry," she whispered.

I struggled to catch my breath and get my heart down out of my throat and back into my chest.

"I didn't mean to startle you," she apologized.

"You didn't startle me, you nearly scared me to death! You shouldn't be here," I hissed at her.

"I had to come after you. You forgot this." She handed me my pocketknife.

"Thanks," I mumbled.

"I thought it might come in handy if you need to cut through the ropes."

"Sure," I said as I stuffed it into one of the front pockets of my jeans. "Now you'd better get back to Andrew . . . quietly."

She nodded and then started off. I waited and listened. I didn't hear a thing except for the crackling of the fire, the waves hitting the shore, and the chirping of the crickets.

Sure that Victoria was safe, I decided it was time to get closer. Dropping to my knees I began to crawl. As I crawled I could feel the knife in my pocket, digging into my leg. I stopped, reached into my pocket and removed it. I'd keep it in my right hand. I had a strange urge to open it up, revealing the blade, like somehow that would protect me. That was totally stupid. What could an eight-centimetre blade do against a man with a gun? All my knife was good for was digging up roots, or cutting a fish . . . or cutting ropes . . . or slicing the back out of a tent . . . the tent where they were being held prisoner.

A burst of electricity surged up my spine. This was no longer about me just getting close enough to have a look and then running away. This was about me going right up to the back of the tent, making an opening, cutting the ropes and leading Ray and Albert to safety. That plan made my head start to spin. Did I really think I could do that? Then again, why not? And if I did, if I was able to free them, then I wouldn't be in charge. Ray or Albert could take over. That thought was stronger than any fear I was feeling.

I chose a route where I could crawl through the shadow of the tent right up to the very edge of the woods. Safe within that shadow I'd be hard to see, even if somebody was looking right at me. I crept forward like I was moving in slow motion, not making a sound. I reached the back of the tent and pressed in as close as I could without actually touching the material. I held my breath and listened. Fire crackling . . . water . . . leaves rustling . . . crickets . . . and breathing. It was coming from the tent. It had to be Ray and Albert.

I peered into the little screen flaps. At first I could see absolutely nothing. Then, little by little, a dark shape started to take form. Then I saw a second body. It had to be them.

"Ray!" I whispered as loud as I dared. There was no answer. "Albert!" I waited. Nothing.

I couldn't risk calling out any louder. I'd have to get closer. I brought my right hand up and opened the blade. I pushed the tip in through the nylon and it easily penetrated. I stopped. Somehow it just didn't seem right to destroy a tent. That was probably the silliest thought I'd ever had. It wasn't like I was doing this for fun.

I started to pull the knife down, holding the tent with my free hand. The blade easily slipped through the material until there was a slit all the way to the ground. I repositioned the knife at the top and began a horizontal cut. The nylon gave way easily and a large triangular flap was created.

I stuck my head into the tent. There was no movement but I could hear them breathing more clearly, and they were slightly more visible because there was a bigger trickle of light coming through the flap. I could see Ray's face. Albert was turned away from me. I took the knife and made the third cut and a new door was created. I crawled into the tent.

It was funny, but I suddenly felt safer. Maybe it was because I was inside the tent and out of view. Maybe it was just being close to Ray. I'd untie him and then he'd take care of everything.

I moved closer to Ray, bent down and put my mouth close to his ear. "Ray . . . Ray." There was no answer. Gently I shook his shoulder and his eyes popped wide open. He looked like I'd woken him from a nightmare, like he was just about to scream out in fear. Then his expression softened.

"Jamie?" he whispered, his voice hoarse and faint and questioning. "Is that you?"

"Yeah, it's me." Of course it was me.

"Are you real?"

What was I supposed to answer to that?

"Is this a dream?" he asked, his voice getting louder.

"No," I whispered. "It's real. I'm real. I'm here to rescue you."

"You are?"

"Ssshhhhh!" I hissed. "Keep your voice down."

He nodded. "I need water . . . do you have any water?"

"Not with me. You can have some as soon as we escape. Let me cut the ropes and—"

Suddenly I was shoved from behind and the whole tent exploded in brightness. I looked back, shielding my eyes with my hands. All I could see was a brilliantly bright flashlight and the tip of a gun pointed at me!

CHAPTER NINETEEN

"DROP YOUR WEAPON!" a voice screamed out.

Weapon? What was he talking about?

"Drop your knife!" he screamed.

Oh, my knife. I let it fall to the ground.

Someone reached in and grabbed me by the front of my shirt. He pulled me up and dragged me away from the tent. His power and my helplessness to resist shocked me. He threw me down to the ground in a heap.

"Where are the others?" he demanded.

I didn't answer.

"Where are the girl and boy?"

I lay there in shock, the bright light still aimed right at me, blinding me. All at once I felt a searing jolt of pain in my side and I was rocketed backwards. He'd kicked me!

"Where are they?" he demanded. "Tell me now before I get angry!" His voice was now quiet and ominous. He took the end of the gun and poked it in my stomach. Didn't he know you should never point a gun at somebody in case it accidentally . . . What was I thinking? Of course he knew that.

"Are you prepared to die for them, boy?" he asked.

"I . . . um . . . um . . ." I stammered. I didn't know what he expected or wanted me to say. I just knew I didn't want him to kick me again.

"You are protecting two members of the ruling class. Do you think that the Royal Family has ever done anything for your people? For the Native people?" he demanded. "They took away your land and exploited your people, just as they have exploited people around the world!"

Again I remained silent, but I thought about his voice, his accent. He sounded just like Albert, or Andrew, or Victoria . . . or Nigel. If I wanted to stay calm, it was probably better not to think about Nigel.

"Your loyalty is admirable, but misguided. Do you think that either one of those children would be so loyal to you? Do you?" he asked as he poked the gun harder into my gut.

"I don't know."

"Well I do!" he snapped. "I'll show you the answer."

He withdrew the gun from my stomach.

"Hello!" he yelled, and I flinched. "I know you're out there. Your friend is my prisoner now!"

There was nothing but silence. It seemed as if even the waves had stopped hitting the shore to listen to what he had to say.

"Your friend is fine . . . but he won't be fine for long!" He paused, and I waited for him to complete that ominous thought. "In fifteen seconds I am going to kill him!"

The hairs on the back of my neck suddenly sprang up.

"That is, if you do not give yourselves up! Do you understand?"

I definitely understood what he meant.

"You are about to see that they are not prepared to sacrifice themselves for you," he said quietly to me.

"But they might not even be close enough to—"

"You'd better hope they are!" he snapped. "Fifteen, fourteen, thirteen, twelve . . ."

This was crazy. He didn't really mean it, did he? This had to be some sort of bluff.

"Eleven, ten, nine—"

"Please, you can't—"

"Quiet!" he snapped.

This wasn't a bluff. He really was going to kill me if they didn't appear, or I didn't tell him where they were. I knew they were probably heading up the creek. I could tell him. I could, but I wasn't going to.

"Eight, seven, six—"

"I'm over here!" Andrew yelled out.

I looked over my shoulder. The flashlight beam was aimed at him. He had just come out of the bushes on the far side of the clearing. His hands were above his head. He moved into the clearing and then stopped.

"Where is the Princess?" the man demanded. "Where is your sister?"

I was wondering that myself. It wasn't like Victoria to quit, she wouldn't have just run away and deserted her brother and me.

"She isn't here," Andrew answered. "She has an injury. I think her leg is broken. Can you help her?"

She must have got hurt when she was trying to get back to him after giving me the knife, I thought.

"Come forward," the man ordered. "And no tricks!"

"Tricks?" Andrew said. "I am too tired and hungry and worn down even to think of tricks. I just wish to surrender." He walked toward us, his hands high above his head.

Then I caught a glimpse of movement in the darkness directly behind the man. It was Victoria! She wasn't hurt after all. Slowly she crept from the shadows. In her hand was a tree limb. She moved closer and closer. I held my breath. She raised the branch over her head and then brought it crashing down! It smashed against his head with a sickening thud, splitting in two, and he collapsed in a heap, almost on top of me!

"Grab his weapon!" Victoria yelled.

I remained frozen to the spot.

"Jamie, get his gun!"

His gun! Of course! I grabbed it from the dirt beside him and jumped to my feet, springing backwards and away from him. The pain in my side, where he'd kicked me, nearly made me double over. But I stood up straight and trained the rifle on him.

"I can't believe you did that," I said to Victoria.

"Neither can I, but it's nothing less than what you would have done for me or for my brother," she said. She was still holding the broken chunk of the limb.

"Is he dead?" Andrew asked.

Just then the man groaned.

"You knocked him out. We'd better tie him up before he comes to," I said.

"Tie him up with what?" Andrew questioned.

"Rope. The ropes that are holding Ray and Albert." I bent down and picked up the flashlight, handing it to Victoria. "Take this. You'll find my knife on the floor in the tent."

"And you'll keep an eye on him?"

"I'll keep more than an eye on him. I'll keep the gun on him."

"Excellent!" She started away and then hesitated. "You do know the workings of that weapon, do you not?"

"I know how to use a gun."

"But that particular type of gun?"

It certainly was different from a regular hunting rifle. It was some sort of assault weapon that I'd only seen in war movies.

"You hurry up and untie them. I'll bet you Albert will know. I'll try and figure it out while you're gone." I paused. "And just to make sure, hand me that piece of wood you're holding."

Victoria looked at the broken-off limb in her hand as though she'd forgotten it was there. She handed it to me and hurried off to the tent. Andrew followed her while I kept one eye on the man and looked at the gun with the other.

It was pretty fancy, but it was still just a rifle. That meant it had a trigger, a magazine for the ammunition, a sight and a safety. Was the safety on? I searched the side of the rifle and found a little toggle switch. Was it on or off? I pressed the button. He must have had it on when he had it aimed at my gut. He wouldn't have risked it going off by accident and killing me—would he? I turned it and examined the ammunition clip. It was big. It had to hold at least thirty or forty bullets. That meant this was some sort of automatic weapon, like a mini machine gun.

Gently I moved my finger to the trigger and the gun exploded, sending a wave of bullets streaming into the ground! The sound was deafening, and I jumped back, partly from fright but partly because of the kick of the gun. I released the trigger and it continued to spray shots for another second. That was amazing . . . how many shots had fired in that two-second burst?

"Jamie!" Victoria screamed. "Are you—?"

"I'm okay!" I hollered back. "Everything is under control! Keep working!"

I looked down at the man and was shocked to see him looking up at me. In the dim light thrown by the dying fire I couldn't see very well, but I could tell that he was semi-conscious. The sound of the gunfire must have roused him. Well, at least now I knew how to fire the gun if I needed to. A burst from that gun wouldn't have just stopped him; it would have cut him in two. I took another step back.

"Hurry up!" I screamed.

"We're coming!" Victoria called.

Ray, an arm around Andrew, and then Albert, supported by Victoria, stumbled out of the tent. There was no telling how long it had been since they'd been allowed to walk, and they were struggling badly. Almost on cue Ray dropped to the ground, pulling Andrew down on top of him.

"Are you all right?"

"They're both a bit unsteady on their feet," Victoria said. "They've been given no food and barely any water since they were captured. Andrew, bring them some water!"

Andrew got to his feet and grabbed a pot that was sitting by the fire. He ran down to the water's edge, plunged the pot in, then charged back, the water splashing over the side of the pot as he ran. He brought it over to Ray, who took the pot with both hands and began to drink greedily, water pouring down his face.

"Not too much or too fast," Albert croaked. "Slowly, or you will become sick and throw it all back up."

Ray lowered the pot and took a smaller sip. He then handed it to Albert, who began to drink.

Ray staggered to his feet. "Jamie," he said slowly. "You're okay . . . But what about those other men?"

"They're far away. We led them most of the way to McGregor's fishing lodge before we doubled back to rescue you and Albert."

"You had this planned all along?" Albert asked in amazement.

"Jamie had a general idea of what to do," Victoria said. "He kept us safe. We just followed his direction."

"Except for that last part," Andrew said. "That was Victoria's idea."

"But I only did what Jamie would have done in the same situation," Victoria added.

It was kind of her to say that, but I wasn't so sure I would have had either the brains to think through a plan that fast . . . or the guts to follow through.

"What are we going to do with him?" Ray asked.

"I have the ropes that bound you and Albert. We were planning on tying him up," Victoria said.

"Here, let me do it," Ray said. "I know a few things about knots. I'll tie him up real good."

"Are you all right to do that?" I asked. "How about you hold the gun and I'll do it."

Ray shook his head. "It's not safe for me to hold a gun on him." He paused. "I'd just kill him." Suddenly Ray reached out and kicked the man in the shoulder. He groaned in pain, and Ray practically tumbled over. He regained his balance and looked like he was getting ready to boot him again.

"Ray, don't!" Albert yelled.

"I still owe him a half dozen more for the times he kicked and slapped me and you when we were tied up!"

Not to mention the time he kicked me just now, I silently added.

Albert put a hand on Ray's shoulder. "I know how you feel. Exactly how you feel. But we cannot allow ourselves to sink to the level of these animals. They only win when we allow ourselves to become like them."

I looked at Ray. His face was twisted and angry. I'd never seen Ray look like that, and it was frightening.

Was he going to listen or . . . ? He stepped back, away from the man.

"Good chap," Albert said, slapping him on the back. "I will tie him up while you get some food. I believe there is something by the fire, but again, as with the water, eat slowly."

Ray walked away on unsteady feet.

Albert took the pieces of rope from Victoria. He stooped down beside the man and grabbed his hands, trying to pull them behind his back. The man, who was now more conscious, resisted.

"Jamie," Albert called out. "I am too weak to wrestle with this fellow. I would prefer to bring him to justice, but if he does not co-operate now, if he fights me, I want you to shoot him." He said the words so calmly, in a matter-of-fact way, like he was just saying I should get the guy a coffee.

"The way this thing is set I can't shoot him once, but I can guarantee I can put fifteen bullets into him in a split second."

"One would be sufficient. There is a small knob on the left-hand side, just above the trigger."

That was the button I'd clicked. "You mean the safety?"

"The safety is on the other side of the stock, farther down. That is the toggle that changes the gun from automatic to single shot. Please click it."

That meant two things. It had been set to take only one shot, and the safety had already been off when he'd had the gun stuck in my gut. I clicked the little button.

"I'm ready to shoot," I said.

I don't know if I really could have shot him, but he seemed pretty sure I would. He allowed Albert to pull his hands behind his back. Albert yanked the rope tight and the man grimaced. Next Albert turned him over on his belly and bound his feet together with a second piece of rope. He double-checked the tightness of the rope and the knot. When he was done, I lowered the gun.

"Now if somebody would help me to my feet I believe that I should also have something to eat. It's been over two days since I had any food."

Both Victoria and Andrew offered him a hand and pulled him up.

"I don't imagine that the three of you have eaten much either, have you?" Albert asked.

"Not a lot," Andrew said.

"I see," Albert said. "Then, Jamie, give me the weapon and I'll stand watch while you eat."

"I've had lots of berries, and some roots and all the water I needed. You eat and I'll get something after."

"No, no, I insist," Albert said.

"You can insist all you want. Until you and Ray have eaten and had enough to drink I'm going to stand guard. We need to get you strong enough to travel."

"You might as well eat, Albert," Victoria said. "Jamie is nothing if not stubborn."

"This coming from you!" I snapped.

"At least I am reasonable enough to admit that I can, at times, be stubborn—unlike some people, who are too stubborn even to admit it—"

"Both of you knock it off!" Ray demanded. "You sound like an old married couple!"

That shut us both up.

"All of you eat and I'll watch him," Ray said.

"You? Is that safe?"

"Sure, give me the gun, and don't worry. I'm not going to kill him. I'm not even going to kick him again—unless he gives me a reason."

Reluctantly I handed the gun to Ray. The attraction of eating outweighed any fear I had about him doing something he shouldn't do. Besides, this was Ray. Trustworthy, good old Ray. And if I wasn't mistaken, I thought I smelled baked beans.

CHAPTER TWENTY

I WOKE WITH A START and sat bolt upright. I was in the tent and Ray was right beside me. He was asleep, a whistling sound coming out of his nose with each breath he exhaled. For a split second I had the strange thought that I'd just woken from a very bad dream. Then I saw the back of the tent, cut open and held in place by a few pins.

Ray continued to sleep at my side, but I knew it hadn't been an easy sleep. He'd moaned and groaned and turned and fussed all night. Twice he'd even woken me up when he'd called out. Both times I'd told him that he was safe, that everything was okay and he could go back to sleep.

I wanted to get up, but Ray was blocking the door. I didn't want to risk waking him now that he was finally sleeping peacefully. I figured I'd just use the "back door." I undid three of the pins and the flap opened up enough for me to slip out.

I stood up and was surprised to see Victoria sitting by the dying embers of the campfire. She was holding the rifle and watching our prisoner, who was still lying on his belly on the ground.

"Good morning!" I called out. "I didn't expect to see you on guard duty."

"Albert looked exhausted, so I though it best to relieve him."

"How about if I relieve you?"

"That would be good." She awkwardly handed me the gun. I was grateful that the safety was on.

I looked down at the man—and he was glaring back at me. I stepped back.

"We have to leave soon," I said.

"Do you think Albert and Ray will be able to travel?" she asked.

"They can both sit in the bottom of a canoe, but I don't know how much paddling either one of them will be able to do," I admitted.

"I wonder as well. They're still very weak."

"Why wouldn't he feed them, or at least give them water?" I asked.

"Because these are the tactics used by terrorists around the world."

I turned around at the sound of Albert's voice. He was awake, and looking slightly better than he had the night before.

"Terrorists?" I asked.

"It's a technique to keep the captives alive to use as bargaining chips, while leaving them disoriented and too weak to escape," he explained.

"That's awful," Victoria said. "That's so cruel, so immoral."

"Such people are immoral."

"Who do you think he works for?" Victoria asked.

"I do not know. I tried to question him while I was

standing guard. He says nothing."

The man smirked.

"All I know is that he and his associates are all English."

"English!" Victoria exclaimed. "He is one of us?"

"Not one of us, but definitely English. I heard them speaking, and their accents could not be mistaken."

"But why would our own countrymen want to do this?" Victoria asked.

"I cannot answer that," Albert said. "But answers will be found once we have him in custody. He can refuse to talk, but using fingerprints, retinal scans, intelligence reports and photographs we will soon know both his identity and who he is aligned with."

The man laughed. It was an evil sound.

"You don't think we can identify you?" Albert asked.

"I don't think you will be bringing me anywhere," he said.

He'd spoken!

"So you found your tongue," Albert said.

"I can speak if I choose."

"And do you choose to tell us why we will not be bringing you to justice?"

"Because I'm not going anywhere."

"That's where you're wrong. We shall soon be breaking camp and you will be accompanying us."

"That's where *you* are wrong," he said. "I refuse to move, and I don't believe that you'll be able carry me far."

He was right. Even in pairs we couldn't very well carry him on the portage. Maybe Albert could have made a good attempt at that a few days ago, but now he could barely carry his own weight.

"I have a gun," Albert said as he took the weapon from my hands. "You will co-operate or I will be forced to shoot you."

The man looked at the gun, and then up at Albert. "Go ahead."

Albert clicked off the safety and brought the gun up, aiming it squarely at the man's chest. Was he really going to shoot him?

"You're bluffing, and we both know it," the man said calmly. "You won't shoot me."

Slowly Albert lowered the gun.

"You are too *civilized,* too *moral,* too *proper* to shoot a man lying on the ground. It would go against all your training as a member of the *famous* British Secret Service." The man laughed again.

"Maybe it goes against his training, but not against mine!" Ray said as he appeared from behind me. "Here, give me the gun and I'll shoot him!"

I grabbed Ray by the arm as he came by me. I was shocked when I not only stopped him dead in his tracks, but also practically pulled him off his feet. I had to use both hands to steady him.

"You can't do that, Ray."

Ray just glared. It was beginning to look like a standoff.

"You're all too weak!" the man scoffed. "You're all too weak to shoot me, and that's the difference between us. I would not hesitate. None of you has the guts to do the job!"

What was with this guy, did he want to get somebody mad enough to shoot him?

"I am a man and you are all nothing but a bunch of
little schoolgirls!"

"Schoolgirls? You mean, like her?" I asked, pointing at
Victoria.

"Exactly!"

"That's real nice of you to compliment us like that.
That schoolgirl outwitted your three friends and then
came back here and captured you, armed with only a
piece of wood when you had an assault weapon. Quite
a schoolgirl, eh?" I asked.

"That's right!" Ray exclaimed. "He was captured by
the person he was trying to capture! He was outwitted,
out-manoeuvred and overpowered by a thirteen-year-
old *princess*!"

Albert started to laugh.

"No wonder he doesn't want to come back with us.
He'd be the laughingstock of the criminal world! I can
just see the headlines, 'Kidnapper Knocked
Unconscious by Princess!'"

"Shut up!" the man screamed.

"Aw, what's wrong with the poor baby?" Ray taunted
him. "Be good or we'll have the little Princess deal with
you again. Are you afraid of her?"

"I am not afraid of any of you, least of all Torie!"

Torie! The laughter died in my throat. He'd called
her Torie. The only place she was known as Torie was on
the Internet!

"His name is Leslie," I said, my voice barely above a whisper. "Or at least that's the name he uses in the chat rooms."

"Oh my goodness," Victoria gasped. "You . . . you think . . . ? No, that cannot be."

The man's face broke into a satisfied smirk. "Would Torie like to talk about clothes, or her favourite pop music group, or perhaps her horses or television?"

"What is he babbling on about?" Albert asked.

Victoria didn't answer, and I wouldn't answer for her.

"Didn't you wonder how we arrived when we did? I've been talking to our little Torie on the Internet for months. Talking, gathering information, gaining her trust. Me knowing exactly who she was, but her thinking that I was a thirteen-year-old girl!" He started to laugh again.

"Who do you work for?" Albert demanded.

"I work for myself," he answered, "and nobody else."

"Then why were you trying to kidnap the Prince and Princess?" Albert asked.

He shrugged. "It had nothing to do with politics, I can assure you."

"Then what?" I asked.

"It was about money," he said.

Albert scoffed. "Did you really think that you could kidnap them, demand a ransom and hope to escape afterward?"

"No. Our plan was not to ransom them back to their family. We were going to sell them to the highest bidder. Whichever extremist group wanted them the most had only to provide the highest bid."

"Bid . . . like an auction?" I asked.

"There was going to be an auction for a very select group of organizations . . . on the Internet."

"Why are you telling us all of this?" Victoria asked.

"Why not?" he answered.

"We have to leave!" Albert exclaimed, jumping to his feet.

"Are you giving up so easily?" the man asked. "There is so much information I have that you need to know. Information you will never get once you leave this camp."

"Everybody. We have to leave immediately!" Albert snapped.

"Can't we have breakfast first?"

"No! This man has been giving us information in an effort to distract us, to keep us here. He knows that the others are returning, and soon!"

Those words froze me to the spot. I had a sudden vision in my head of the three of them, weapons ready, creeping through the bushes, surrounding us as we stood there in the clearing.

"What do you want us to do?" I asked.

"Victoria, wake up your brother, and then the two of you must gather all the food you can find and put it into two backpacks. Ray, check to make sure our prisoner remains well bound. Jamie, break down two tents and gather just the essential equipment."

"Right, sure. Let's go!" I said.

We all scrambled around the campsite. I ripped the pegs out of the ground, grabbed the tent and dumped the contents onto the ground. I balled the tent up and stuffed it into its carrying bag. Next I stuffed that into a pack. I went to grab a sleeping bag and then stopped. It would be better to travel light, even if it meant sleeping without the bags. Next I grabbed the hammer and the axe and went to put them in the pack.

"Leave the hatchet out!" Albert called.

"We should bring it with us," I argued.

"Perhaps, but you have to use it before we go."

"You want me to cut up more wood for him?" I asked in amazement.

Albert shook his head. "They arrived in two canoes. They are just over there, hidden in the bushes. I want you to take the axe and destroy them."

"Destroy them!"

"Yes. I don't want to give them any opportunity to come after us."

"Speaking of canoes," Ray said, "where's my third canoe?"

I was still dreading telling him what had happened. I hesitated.

"It's in a secure place," Victoria said. "We can't get to it right now, but neither can anybody else."

She certainly wasn't lying about that. Nobody was going to be using that canoe for a long time, if ever.

"That leaves us two canoes. That's probably better anyway," Ray said. "We can all fit, and that'll make it easier to portage around the rapids. Jamie, you go and destroy those canoes and I'll finish up here. Better for me to decide what needs to come with us."

I started toward the canoes, and then I came across a sight that took my breath away. Something was wrapped in a blue canvas that stuck out of the ground—something the size of a man's body. It was Nigel.

"What's the matter, Jamie?" Ray asked.

Luckily, the others were distracted. I walked right beside Ray. "It's . . . it's Nigel," I whispered. Ray shook his head. "Just leave him, Jamie. We'll send somebody back for the body once we get back home."

I stumbled and dropped my end of the canoe. It fell noisily to the ground. Normally I would have braced myself for Ray yelling at me if I'd dropped one of his precious canoes. This time I knew I had nothing to fear. Both canoes had been dropped a half dozen times— sometimes by Ray himself. Thank goodness we were almost there. I could see the lake just ahead.

This had been the worst portage of my life. Everything—the canoes, the packs, even my own legs— seemed incredibly heavy. Ray, who could normally carry both a canoe and his pack on his back, had barely been able to carry a thing. Albert hadn't been any better. He had staggered and tripped repeatedly. At least the path had been downhill. I don't think we could have managed if we'd been going up instead.

"I think we'd better rest here," Ray said.

"You rest. I'll move the canoe to the water's edge and come back and help."

"You're going to do that by yourself?" Ray asked.

"I'll help too," Victoria offered.

"Are you sure you're able?" Albert wondered.

"I'm fine, Albert," she said. "I am far more worried about you."

He smiled, ever so slightly, and nodded.

"You stay here and we'll be back soon."

I grabbed the canoe and heaved it up right onto my back. I was surprised by just how heavy it seemed, but proud I'd done it anyway.

"Walk beside me," I said to Victoria, "and steady it if it looks like I'm going to fall."

She came up beside me and we started down the path.

"Have you thought about how we are going to travel?" she asked.

"Ray's going to be in the same canoe as you and Andrew. I'll keep Albert with me."

"I imagine that's the only way that makes sense, although I would have liked to share the ride with you. I have so much enjoyed our conversations."

I felt myself blushing. "Me too. But I guess we'll have time to talk when we get back to safety."

"Probably not," she said. "They will whisk me away almost immediately."

"Oh . . . yeah . . . I guess they'll want to make sure you're okay."

"But that doesn't mean that we can't speak. Perhaps we could make phone calls, or even chat on the Inter . . ." She let the sentence trail off. "I would imagine that I will not be having many conversations on the Internet now."

"You didn't know," I said. "You didn't know who he was, and you certainly didn't know that he knew who you were. It's not your fault."

"I have already spent a great deal of time, in my mind, trying to convince myself of that. So far I have not been successful."

I didn't know what to say to that. "Here we are," I said instead. I flipped the canoe off my shoulders with some help from Victoria and dropped it down, easing it into the water. "Let's go back and get the other canoe."

The three of them were still sitting when we arrived. Albert got to his feet. He had the gun slung over his shoulder.

"I'll take the second canoe and the rest of you carry the bags."

No one argued with me. I wasn't sure if I was happy about that or not. I'd had the idea that once we freed Ray and Albert, they'd be in charge. But they still didn't seem like themselves. Great, now instead of being responsible for two people I was responsible for four.

I heaved the second canoe up onto my shoulders and started to walk. Victoria walked along beside me, steadying the canoe. I tried to focus on the path under my feet but instead my mind started to think about how I really would have liked to spend the day with her in my canoe. We could have talked. I guessed that we'd have some time that night at the campsite. But when we finally reached my village, it would probably be like Victoria had said and she'd be gone quickly. I wondered if I'd ever see her again.

Somehow it seemed easier carrying the second canoe than the first. Maybe it was because we were getting closer to the end. Once I put this one in the water all we'd have to do was paddle to safety.

I put the canoe down into the water alongside the first.

"Put the packs in the middle of this one," I said, pointing. "Albert, you're going in the front of it and I'm going in the back."

He nodded.

"And, Ray, I want you in the middle. Andrew is going up front and Victoria will be in the stern."

"I can take the stern," Ray said.

"You can take the stern later if you're feeling better. For now, I want Victoria there. Okay?"

I had expected Ray to put up a fight, but he just nodded weakly in agreement. We stowed the packs in my canoe. Next I helped Andrew and Ray and Victoria climb into the other canoe. I waded into the water and pushed them out. Finally Albert sat down in the bow of our canoe. He placed the rifle on the bottom beside him. I pushed our canoe out and leaped in. I sat down, picked up the paddle and dipped it into the water. It felt good to be on the water again. Somehow it felt safe, leaving those men behind us somewhere in the woods. There was no way they could catch us now.

CHAPTER TWENTY-ONE

I DIPPED THE PADDLE IN DEEP and we glided forward. I was surprised how much power my arms still held. A couple of good meals and some rest had really made a difference. Of course, I'd only gone a few hundred metres. We still had two full days of paddling to look forward to. I'd have to wait and see how my arms felt by then. On the bright side, maybe what Victoria had said was true, and when we didn't return by nightfall they'd send somebody out to find us.

I looked over my shoulder. The other canoe was trailing close behind. Victoria and Andrew weren't doing badly. Certainly a lot better than I would ever have expected from them just a few short days ago. Wow . . . a few days ago was when this had all started. It seemed like years had passed since we'd first set out.

"Jamie!" Victoria called out. I turned around.

"In the bay!" she yelled, pointing off to the side.

I looked into the distance. There, protected from the open water, sitting in a little bay, was a float plane, gently bobbing up and down on the waves. With everything that had happened I'd forgotten about it. That was how they'd flown in. That was how they were going to make their escape. Then another thought hit me right

·

between the eyes. That was also how they could come after us. Paddling across the lake, we'd be completely exposed to anybody flying above us. Even if they didn't leave until tomorrow afternoon they could still catch us long before we reached my village. If they spotted us in open water we'd be sitting ducks. They could land practically on top of us, or even just shoot us from the air.

Albert turned around in his seat. "That plane is a problem."

I nodded in agreement.

"Do you know what we have to do?" he asked.

"No, what?"

"We have to take care of that plane."

"Take care of it?"

"Yes. We have to go over and disable it, make it impossible for them to follow us by air, the way we've already stopped them from following us by water."

"But I left the axe back at the camp," I said. I'd tossed it into the woods, far enough away so that our prisoner couldn't wiggle over and use the blade to cut himself free.

"I thought we might be able to disable it without chopping a hole in the bottom. I imagine you know something about float planes," he said.

"I know a lot."

"Then you would certainly know what we could do to make it inoperable," Albert said.

"I can do that," I agreed.

"Not only do we not want them to follow us, but we also want to cut off their means of escape. Without that plane they will be stranded up here, and the authorities will surely capture them."

"I hadn't even thought of that, but that makes sense."

"Good. Get us over to the plane."

I changed our course, and Victoria, steering the other canoe, followed behind. We came up to the plane and I brought the canoe right up beside one of the floats. It was a beautiful plane, almost new, bigger than my father's. It looked to be a ten-seater. I climbed out onto the float. Albert held onto the float to keep the canoe from drifting. The other canoe came up right behind us.

"This is some beautiful plane," Ray said. "Shame your father isn't here. It would save us two days and a whole lot of paddling."

"I wish he were here," I said. And I wished that for a whole lot of reasons not related to his ability to fly.

"Jamie, how many times have you flown your father's plane?" Ray asked.

"Dozens of times."

"So you could fly this one?"

"He certainly cannot!" Victoria exclaimed.

"I probably *could* fly it, but—"

"He is not going to fly it!" she said. "And if he does, I am not flying in it with him!"

There was no point in taking offence, because what she was saying made sense. "Victoria's right," I agreed. "What I *can* do and what I'm *going* to do are two very different things."

"Could we please just get on with the task at hand?" Albert said. He had tied off the canoe and climbed up onto the float. Andrew and Ray followed suit.

I put my hand on the handle of the door and it popped open. I climbed up the ladder and plopped down in the pilot's seat. What would be the best thing I could do, the simplest thing, to make sure they couldn't fly away? One thing seemed obvious: the key was still in the ignition. I imagined that they hadn't thought that anybody would steal the plane—or the key. I could now just take the key when we left, although that certainly wasn't all I was going to do.

"I think we have to cut the wires that lead down to the rudders. Without those wires they won't even be able to take off. We could also puncture the gas tanks. Without fuel they're not going anywhere."

"That sounds good," Albert said. "How do we go about taking care of those tasks?"

"The best place to get to the wires is through the cockpit. Climb in here and we'll rip them right out, and then—"

There was a high-pitched buzzing sound, followed almost immediately by a bang—a gunshot!

"What the—"

Another shot rang out and the side window exploded!

"Everybody take cover!" Albert shouted.

He practically threw Victoria and Andrew into the cockpit, and Ray followed right behind. Through the open door I could see Albert. He had perched down behind one of the struts and he had the rifle in his hands, aiming it toward shore. Another shot rang out, and another and another. Victoria screamed as another window shattered and glass fragments showered down on us! I wanted to reach out to her, tell her it was going to be okay, but I was just as afraid as she was.

"Attention!" called out a voice. "There is no escape! You have no place to run and no place to hide! You can give yourselves up or we will shoot you . . . we will shoot you all!"

There was silence. I looked down at Albert. "How many of them?"

"All four. Two on the shore to the left about thirty metres away. Two others circling around to the right to get us in a crossfire."

"Can we get in the canoes and get away?" Ray asked.

"Not a chance," he said, shaking his head. "As soon as we get in the canoes they'll cut us down. The only reason they are firing with restraint now is because they do not want to destroy the plane and their means of escape."

"What is your answer!" called out a voice.

Albert shrugged. "We need a minute to decide," he called out.

"You will decide immediately!"

"We need time!" Albert yelled back. "It's not as though we're going anywhere!"

There was no answer, which I assumed meant they were giving us the time we'd asked for—not that I knew what we were going to do with it.

Albert moved to the open door and climbed inside. "Does anyone see any options?" he asked.

Nobody answered.

"What will happen if we surrender?" Ray asked.

Albert said nothing, which I guess did provide an answer.

"That's what I thought," Ray said. "Well, if I'm going to die, I'd rather die trying to get away."

"I agree," Albert said, "although that still does not answer the question of how we will accomplish it."

"I guess I can only think of one thing. Get in the plane," I said quietly.

"You do not mean that you are going to fly this plane!" Victoria gasped.

"Not fly it," I said. "Taxi it away . . . drive it like a motorboat."

"You can do that?" she asked anxiously.

"I can. This thing will go almost forty-five kilometres an hour skimming along the water. All I need are two things. I need some time to check out the controls, make sure it's the same as my father's plane, and then I need somebody to cut the anchor."

"I will get you some time," Albert said. "And I'll try to cut the anchor line at the same time."

"Here, take my knife," I said, handing it to him.

Albert climbed out of the cockpit and crouched down behind the strut. The line to the anchor was right beside him.

"We wish to discuss terms!" Albert yelled out.

"No terms!" came back the reply.

"Just hear me out! It has nothing to do with the Prince or Princess! They will be surrendered to you!"

There was no response, which meant they must have been talking it over. I started to scan the instruments. These were basically the same controls, although some of them were in slightly different places.

"Let us hear your terms!"

Albert didn't answer right away. I looked over and through the open door I could see that he was using my knife to saw away at the anchor line.

"What are the terms?" the voice called out.

Albert leaned into the plane. "How much time do you need?"

"Just a few more seconds," I said. I hit the toggles to feed fuel into the engine.

"The Prince and Princess, accompanied by myself," he yelled, "will come to shore and surrender, but we will do so only after you allow our two guides to paddle away to safety!"

There was no immediate answer. Again they were probably thinking this through.

"Are you ready?" Albert asked as he leaned into the open door.

"Is the anchor gone?"

He showed me the cut line in his hand.

"Then I'm ready."

I pulled a lever to drop the water rudders. I hit the ignition and the engine spun to life. I used the foot-pedals to steer the rudders and revved the engine to pull us away. Albert jumped into the plane and slammed the door closed behind him.

"Everybody get down!" he screamed.

I slumped down in the seat as best I could as shots started to ring out. Albert jumped across the seat and thrust the gun out the already smashed rear window. There was a deafening explosion as he returned fire. A shot shattered the front windscreen and glass fragments sprayed into my face! I recoiled in pain, but in the same instant opened up the throttle, and the engine roared louder. We began to pick up speed. The plane bounced and bucked as we plowed through the waves.

Wind rushed in through the shattered windscreen. I brought a hand up to my face and it came away covered in blood! I opened the throttle up another notch and then pulled back on the stick and the ride suddenly got smooth as I lifted it off the water. We were flying! We were flying! Now, nobody could catch us!

CHAPTER TWENTY-TWO

"I THINK I'VE HAD ENOUGH TO EAT," I said to my grandmother.

"Just have another big spoonful. Here, let me help," she said as she took my spoon and dipped it into the bowl of stew—my *third* bowl of stew.

I was going to argue, but I knew there was no point. I opened my mouth and she shovelled it in. I chewed and swallowed.

"What about Ray?" I asked. "He's eaten less than me."

She turned to face Ray and he shot me a dirty look. "I've had plenty, honest, I'm heavier now than I was when I left!"

I got up from the table and brought my bowl to the sink. I looked out the window. On the widest section of the beach a Sikorsky army helicopter had set down. It had brought up two dozen specially equipped soldiers. It was sitting just up from where my father's plane was usually anchored. He was out with the RCMP officers trying to chase down the bad guys.

There was a knock on the door.

"I'll get it," I called out. I went to the front door, opened it, and there stood Albert.

"Hello, Jamie. We were getting ready to leave and Victoria was hoping you would come to see us off."

"Of course I'll come." I turned around. "Going out for a while!" I hollered.

I followed Albert and we headed for the beach. They were apparently being flown out aboard the Sikorsky.

"Did they find those men?" I asked.

"All of them. They were captured and are being transported right now to the air force base in Cold Water, Alberta. From there they will be extradited back to England to face trial."

"That's great. So, my father's safe now . . . right?"

"Very."

I took a deep breath. There was something I wanted to say to Albert.

"I wanted to tell you . . . tell you how sorry I am . . . about Nigel. I really liked him."

"Yes, I will miss him too. We were assigned to the Royal Family together for almost five years and we'd become very good friends. I both liked and respected him. He'll be buried with full military honours, as befitting someone who sacrificed his life for the Crown." Albert stopped walking and faced me. "My biggest regret is that he died before knowing that the Prince and Princess were saved . . . largely because of you."

"We all worked together or it wouldn't have happened."

"Many of us played parts, but you were the one who made all those parts work as a whole. Have you ever thought of a future in the secret service?"

"Me, in the secret service?" I exclaimed. "All I want to do is become a bush pilot, like my father."

"Ahhh, like father, like son. I followed in my father's footsteps, too."

"He was in the secret service?" I asked.

Albert nodded. "One of the proudest days of his life was when I received my commission. I'm sure your father will be proud of you when you become a pilot." He smiled. "Actually, I am sure he is very proud of you right now."

"Proud and angry. He said if I ever tried to fly a plane again before I got my pilot's licence he'd shoot me *himself*!"

Albert burst into laughter. He had a great, big, round laugh, just like my father's. When I'd first met Albert I'd figured he didn't even know *how* to laugh.

"I don't know. Your takeoff was very smooth," Albert said.

"Thanks, but I think I have a little work to do on the landings." I had brought us in too hard and fast and had managed to damage one of the floats, bend the prop— it had dipped into the water—and I'd almost run out of lake before it finally came to a stop, less than ten metres from the shore.

"I once heard it said that any landing that you can walk away from is a good landing. Oh, there's Victoria."

She was partially hidden behind a cluster of soldiers. Each soldier was dressed in battle fatigues with a helmet, and each held an assault weapon like the one I'd been handling. Victoria saw us and waved. She flashed a wonderful smile. She was dressed in new, clean clothes, her hair was washed and styled, and it even looked as though she'd put on a little makeup. Was she wearing lip gloss?

"I was afraid you wouldn't come to say goodbye," she said.

"I didn't know you were leaving already."

"We were scheduled to leave thirty minutes ago, but I said I was not departing until I had seen you," she said.

I didn't know what to say in response, but her words made me feel all gooey inside.

"Albert, could you please arrange for Jamie and me to have some privacy?" she asked.

He nodded. "Attention, please. I would like the guard detail to take a much wider perimeter position."

The soldiers instantly responded, fanning out so that they were still surrounding the Princess but were a couple of dozen metres away in all directions.

"Is that more suitable?" Albert asked.

"Almost perfect," she said. "Though I had wanted to talk to Jamie alone, *completely* alone."

Albert looked as embarrassed as I felt. He scurried away and joined the soldiers on the perimeter.

"How are you feeling, Jamie?"

"Tired, but okay. You?"

"It's strange, but now that it's all over I feel as though it never happened, as if life is exactly the same now as it was before."

"I know exactly what you mean. It's all sort of like a dream," I said.

"Or a nightmare."

"Or a nightmare," I agreed.

"Yet the strange part is that while it is over, I am certain that it has changed me forever."

"You'll get over it. My grandmother says time heals all wounds," I offered.

"I don't want to get over it. My life has been changed, and that change has not only made me different, but stronger, even better. Does that make any sense?"

I thought about what she'd said. I'd been thinking some of the same things, but they were confused, and now that she'd spoken them I understood exactly. "Actually I do."

"I just knew you would, because it is not just me who has been changed. All of us are different, and the difference will never really go away," she said.

I did feel different. I felt older. It was almost like the week before I'd been a kid and now I was a . . . an older, wiser kid.

"I also wanted to thank you again," she said.

"You've done that a dozen times already."

"Then I want to make it a dozen plus one."

"Hey, I should be thanking *you* for coming out into that clearing and smashing that guy in the head and saving my life. That was just about the bravest thing I could ever imagine anybody doing."

"I could not have done that a few weeks ago."

"I don't know about that. You always looked pretty brave to me."

"*Looking* brave and *being* brave are very different things. How does your head feel?"

"Okay. That army doctor took out the pieces of glass and took care of the biggest cut. It took five stitches to close it."

"I hope it will not leave a scar," she said, then she reached out a hand and very gently touched my forehead.

I wanted to say something to her, to tell her how pretty she was, but I couldn't.

"Where's Andrew?" I finally blurted out. That probably wasn't what she'd expected as an answer.

"He's already aboard the helicopter. I believe he's sleeping."

"I can relate to that. I think I could sleep for a month."

"I hope not quite that long, because you will soon be receiving an invitation. You and your parents and grandparents and, of course, Ray."

"What's the invitation for?" I asked.

"To come to London."

"London, England?"

"That *is* where it's located," she chuckled. "Well, I know you have a city called London in Ontario, but it was the English one I had in mind," she teased. "You will be our guests at a ceremony."

"What sort of ceremony?"

"One in which you and Ray will be honoured for your bravery. My father wishes to bestow his thanks upon you formally."

"Does my grandmother know that she's going to meet your father, that she's going to England?"

"Not yet."

"She's going to go out of her mind!"

"And you?"

"And me what?" I asked.

"Are you happy that you'll be coming to England?"

"Yeah, of course I am. It'll be great to see London."

The helicopter's engine came to life and the blades began slowly to spin.

"I believe that's a signal that it is time for me to depart," Victoria said.

"I guess you're right."

"I had better be going," she said. "I just need to thank you—"

"You've already thanked me, and—"

"Will you just shut your mouth for *one* minute?" she snapped. "I still want to offer my thanks, just one more time."

She flung her arms around my neck and pressed her lips against mine and kissed me! I was so shocked that for a split second I didn't close my eyes or kiss back. Then I did both. My lips were against hers and I kissed her back. Finally she let go.

"There, now you have been *properly* thanked. I'll look forward to seeing you in a few weeks."

With that, she turned and ran toward the helicopter, where Albert was waiting to help her aboard. She turned and waved and then disappeared inside. Albert smiled and gave me a little salute and climbed in after her. The big door was pulled up and closed.

I stood there and watched as the rotors turned faster

and faster and faster. The noise was deafening, and I had to turn my head to shield my face from the grit and stones and twigs that were being thrown up into the air. The helicopter lifted off and the sound and fury got even louder, and then it quickly began to fade. It got higher and higher and started flying away. I watched as it receded into the distance and finally disappeared from view. And looking up into the endlessly blue sky, remembering that kiss from a beautiful princess, with everything I had to look forward to, I really did feel as if the world was opening up to me.